JOURNEY TO FREEDOM

BOOK II OF THE WIVES QUARTET

Jay DeMoir

DeMoir Publishing

An Imprint of House of DeMoir Productions

Jay DeMoir

Also by Jay DeMoir

The Wives Quartet:

The Wives

Journey to Freedom

Across the Stars

ISBN-13: 978-1797092775

Disclaimer: This is a work of fiction. Names, characters, places, and incidents are either the product of the author's imagination or are used fictitiously, and any resemblance to actual persons, living or dead, business establishments, or events is entirely coincidental.

JOURNEY TO FREEDOM

Book II of The Wives Quartet

By: Jay DeMoir

Edited by Mrs. MeMee of DeMoir Publishing

&

RaKesha Gray of RGEdits

Dramatis Personae:

The Wives

I. ***Rachel "Rae" Richards***- Homemaker; Widow of Jack Richards—former quarterback in the NFL; 32, Caucasian American.

II. ***Prudence "Prue" Sanchez-Cameron***- Supermodel; estranged wife of Donatello Cameron; 28, Colombian American.

III. ***Rain Fres***- Real estate agent; wife of Derrick Fres; 27, Black British.

IV. ***Freya Goodchild***- Former CIA operative; quit her job to become a homemaker; wife of Aaron Goodchild; mother of five; 32, African American.

V. ***Miranda Copeland***- Botanist; secret widow of George Copeland, whom she murdered; mother of six-year-old Piper Michelle Copeland; 30, Euro-Canadian American.

Their Men

I. ***Donatello Cameron***- Kingpin of an East-coast based crime syndicate; 42, Italian American.

II. ***Derrick Fres***- Record Producer employed by Star BMG; 33, African American.

III. ***Aaron Goodchild***- Partner at Goodchild Law Firm; 39, Caucasian American.

IV. ***Romeo "Ro" Lupe'***- Prue's lover; male model; Mid-20s, French.

Chapter 1

❧ ❧ ❧ ❧ ❧ ❧ ❧ ❧ ❧ ❧ ❧

March 14, 2007

"Romeo!" she cried out, clawing at the sheets. Her body arched away from the torture of his tongue. She'd forgotten what he could do to her. She'd forgotten how he could light her body afire with just his tongue.

Romeo Lupe' wrapped his hands around her thighs and spread them even more as his mouth took in her throbbing sex.

Prudence Sanchez-Cameron gasped in pleasure as his tongue moved over her clitoris. She felt her legs trembling and knew she was close to exploding. She brushed her elbow-length dark hair over her shoulder and gasped as Romeo ran a hand over her tanned skin.

Romeo glanced up at her and grinned. Then he dove back between her thighs and took her into his mouth.

In the next moment, she shook her head and rode the wave as she came. Her long dark hair fell over her breasts as she arched her back again, forcing his tongue deeper into her.

Prue reached down and moved her hands through Romeo's thick curly hair. He was perfect to her. His skin was sweat slicken right now but normally sun-kissed. He was French but she knew that his father had been born in Greece. Mr. Lupe' had to have migrated to France at some point since Romeo was born there. Prue wasn't sure where his mother was from, but wherever she was from she'd produced one chiseled son.

His nose was straight and masculine, and his jawline was darkened by a five o'clock shadow.

Prue gasped as he sucked on her clitoris again and pushed her thoughts aside. She seized the model's head in her hands and held him to her, moving her hips to his mouth.

But Romeo simply restrained her, his breath hot against her flesh. He sucked her folds gently and she cried out. He chuckled and lifted his face from her sex, glancing at her. He smiled, and she felt herself melt.

He was beyond gorgeous! There was no doubt that he'd earned his spot atop the list of the highest paid models—but then again, she'd earned her spot, too. Prudence was a knockout—tall and lean, but curvy in all the right places. She was known as the Colombian Goddess in the modeling realm.

That was how they'd met—as co-workers on a photoshoot so long ago.

Yes, he was handsome and his body was perfect. He was everything she'd ever wanted. But—

Romeo dove back between her thighs and she exhaled, throwing her head back into her pillow.

Thoughts rushed through Prue's mind as Spanish left her lips; words she knew he wouldn't understand as he only spoke French and English with a thick accent.

"Say it in English, my love," he urged her, moving to kiss her. Their lips met and Prue wrapped her arms around his neck.

With one stroke, he slid into her, feeling how wet she was. Prue inhaled sharply and pulled him closer. Sweat dripped from his face and he groaned in pleasure as he moved inside of her—wonder taking hold of him.

Prue then thought about why she'd visited him in the first place. It wasn't to have sex with him, even though she loved when their bodies met in this complicated dance.

No. Prudence had flown to Paris and ended up on the doorstep to his apartment for *answers*.

She needed to know if it was Romeo who had given her HIV…or her husband, Donatello.

Less than twenty-four hours ago, her doctor had informed her that she was HIV positive.

She and Romeo had used condoms, but only in the beginning.

Yes, he'd asked her if she was on the pill, but that only prevented her from getting pregnant. That didn't keep her from contracting any sexually transmitted diseases…

Then her thoughts turned to her husband. She and Donatello hadn't used condoms since they'd gotten engaged. That had been years ago.

She didn't know who Donatello spent his time with on his numerous business trips. He could be carrying on countless affairs behind her back. She couldn't be sure until she confronted him, but he hadn't answered any of her calls or texts. Her husband was pure trash.

Why did we even get married in the first place? She thought to herself as her thoughts continued to pull her away from the present moment.

She looked at Romeo. His eyes were closed, and his face was twisted in pleasure. Even now, as Romeo took her, he'd slid in her unsheathed.

No. Prudence had come to his apartment for *answers*! Unfortunately, he'd opened the door dressed in only a towel—fresh from the shower—and Prudence had lost her anger. She'd rushed into his arms and kissed him and the next thing she knew, she was in his bed, naked, and he was tasting her.

Romeo was so hard, like stone, and moved in rhythmic blows against her pelvis.

Her nails were grasping at his sweat-slicken back, feeling the muscles as his body moved. She suddenly felt her thoughts shift and she instantly felt detached from the moment. Her mind left her body and she felt herself float up as she wondered if this man had given her HIV.

Suddenly, she felt the wetness in her sex begin to dry up, but undoubtedly Romeo hadn't noticed yet.

"No," she whispered, trying to push him away.

He continued to stroke inside her, gasping and moaning. He thrusted hard, groaned, and she could feel him throbbing inside her as he came.

"No!" she shouted, startling him.

Romeo looked at her, shock etched on his face. "*Mon amour?*"

"No! Stop!" she cried. "Get off of me!"

Romeo slid out of her and moved across the bed, confused. "What? What did I do? Is something wrong?"

Prue pulled a sheet up and over her breasts, hiding herself from him as she began to pant. "YOU!" she shouted. He reached out to touch her and she slapped his hand away.

"Prue, what's wrong?" he asked, his face twisting in confusion.

She slapped him across the face and his head turned with the blow. "You unimaginable bastard!"

Romeo rubbed his jaw and looked at her. "What did I do?"

"You screwed me, that's what!" she shouted, throwing pillows at him. Romeo moved off the bed and dodged the pillows.

Prue climbed out of bed and felt tears welling up. She'd come to Paris for answers, but she couldn't even be around him right now. She had to leave, she had to get away from him.

How could she have been so weak?! She'd just found out she was HIV positive and she'd surrendered her body to him. What kind of a monster was she?

Was *he* a monster, too?

She grabbed her clothes and moved towards the door, pulling them on as she did so. She suddenly felt dirty and began to sob.

What was she doing here? Why had she let him have sex with her? She was HIV positive now! Her life would never be the same! What if he wasn't the one who'd infected her? What if it had been Donatello?

What if she'd just exposed Romeo to the disease?

What if? What if? WHAT IF?

Romeo moved after her, asking questions and trying to figure out what was wrong.

She grabbed her Dolce & Gabbana purse and moved towards the door.

He touched her, and she cringed.

"I'm sorry. I can't be here right now." She couldn't look at him. She couldn't face him.

She'd come to Paris to confront him, but now wasn't the time. She rushed out of the apartment, pulling her shirt down as she headed for the stairs.

"Prue!" Romeo called, standing naked in the doorway.

Prue rushed down the winding staircase and out into the city streets.

Fresh air hit her face and she gasped, tears streaming down her cheeks. Wind blew her raven colored hair and she brushed it aside.

She had to get out of Paris. She had to get to the airport. She had to get home. No, she *needed* to get home.

Right now all she needed was her bed. Right now all she needed was the silence of her empty house.

She hailed a taxi and one pulled up to the curb. She told the driver to take her to the airport and she wiped her tears away.

The cab driver eyed her curiously but didn't say anything.

Suddenly, her cellphone began to ring. She rolled her eyes, knowing it was Romeo calling her. She dug the phone out of her purse and looked at the caller ID. It wasn't Romeo, but Miranda— one of her best friends.

She started to ignore the call, but then felt a pang of guilt. She couldn't ignore Miranda; she'd been through so much in recent months.

Prue sniffled and answered the call. "This is Prudence," she said.

"Prue?" came the voice of Miranda. "Are you alright? You sound weird."

Prue smiled despite herself. Miranda always knew when something was wrong, even when she tried to hide it. "It's been a rough day." Prue gazed out the window and caught sight of a couple strolling down the sidewalk holding hands. She swallowed hard and wondered if she'd ever have that kind of companionship now that she had HIV.

"Do you want to talk about it?" asked Miranda.

Prue shook her head then remembered that she was on the phone. Miranda couldn't see her. "I don't want to talk about it…not yet, but hopefully soon."

"Where are you?" Miranda asked, and Prue could hear the worry in her voice.

"Headed to the airport," Prue replied honestly. "I'll be home in ten hours."

"Good," Miranda said. "The funeral's tomorrow…"

Prue swallowed hard. She'd been so wrapped up in her own drama that she'd forgotten all about another of her neighbor's tragedy. Rachel Richards wasn't just Prue's neighbor, but her dear friend. She'd first met Rachel—the perky red head that lived on the same street she did, Lyfe Road—when she and Donatello had first moved into their Craftsman-styled home all those years ago. Rachel had lost her husband, famed NFL player Jack Richards, just the other day.

Prue sighed. Everything had gone so horribly wrong in all her friends' lives. So much had changed for them. They'd all been happy once upon a time and now…life had come at them hard.

Life was unforgiving. Life was tumultuous. Life was a bitch.

Prudence couldn't speak for the others, but she knew she was restless. She was a restless wife…and she couldn't take it anymore.

She was tempted to simply open the door of the cab and roll out of the vehicle and into oncoming traffic.

"Prue, are you still there?" came Miranda's voice, bringing her back to the here and now.

Prue took her hand off the door handle and pressed the phone to her ear. She couldn't believe she'd come so close to giving up on her life. "Yes, I'm still here. I'll be home in time for the funeral, Miranda. I wouldn't dare miss it."

"Good," said Miranda. "Rachel needs us all right now."

I need everyone, too, she thought to herself. "I wouldn't dream of letting Rachel down." And Prue realized that she'd spoken the truth. She just wished she hadn't let herself down…

Back in the States, Miranda Copeland, née Jordan, ended the call and placed her cellphone back in her pocket. She stood in the hallway of a plain building.

Miranda wore jeans and a simple purple shirt. She was slender and had fair skin. Her brunette hair was pulled back in a messy ponytail. She rubbed her hands together and then headed back into the room where eight other women sat in a circle.

"I'm sorry about that," she said, taking her seat.

A somber women looked at her and one muttered an *'it's okay.'*

An older woman with mingle gray hair looked around the circle and locked eyes with Miranda. "Actually, sweetie, it's your turn."

Miranda looked at the African American woman, shock etched on her face. She shook her head and hands at the same time. "No, I'm ok. I just came to observe today. I'm not ready to share."

Miranda had come to this domestic violence group at the urging of her dear friend Freya, but she wasn't sure how much she was willing to share. She was still working through her emotions on her own.

For one, she wasn't a victim anymore. George was—

"It's okay to share," said the Asian woman to Miranda's right, pulling Miranda from her thoughts. Miranda looked at her and the woman grinned at her. "We aren't going to judge you here."

The other women murmured in agreement. Miranda exhaled and rose to her feet. "Well, okay." Her heart began to race, and she cleared her throat, suddenly nervous. She'd never voiced her abuse aloud to strangers before. She didn't count the police she'd reported the abuse to in the past as strangers.

By now, she knew most of those police officers by name. They were like family, only the type of family that never came to her assistance. They'd just stood by and watched until George had gone too far…when he'd knocked Miranda out and she'd fallen into a coma.

Miranda tucked a loose strand of hair behind her ear and looked at the floor. "Hi, I'm Miranda."

"Chin up, honey," the African American woman told her. She seemed to be the facilitator here. "You don't have to be ashamed."

Miranda nodded and looked up. She exhaled again and suddenly felt emotions gather inside of her. Her face felt warm and she knew she was about to speak her truth. "My name is Miranda. I was married—*am* married"—she had to remind herself that no one knew George was dead, but her—"to an abusive man. Well, I guess I could say I *was* married to an abusive man." She looked around the room. "I've finally gotten away."

Around the room, the women began to clap and grin. Miranda smiled shyly.

She gained strength from their support and decided to be honest. "We're separated now… I'm not very sure where he is though. All I know is that we were married for nearly seven years and for more than *five* of those years, I was abused." Miranda suddenly began to recall the first time George had struck her. Her eyes glazed over as she recalled the memories and her eyes grew distant as she stared off—her memories pulling her to the past. "The first time George hit me was when I came home from a business trip. It was my first case as a botanist and he didn't believe I'd actually been away on business. He assumed I was having an affair. He grabbed me by the throat and slammed me against the wall."

Miranda heard an intake of breath but didn't stop. As she began to share, she felt a weight lift off her.

"George choked me until I grew dizzy. He screamed and tightened his grip until I nearly lost consciousness." She took a moment to collect herself, because she was about to reveal a pivotal moment in her life. "I…I was going to leave him right then and there, but I didn't. It took me a moment to pick myself up off the floor. I'd come home from the trip excited to see him because while I was away, I realized that I was pregnant."

A tear escaped her eye and she quickly wiped it away. Saying it out loud after all these years made Miranda feel stupid. She was pregnant with Piper and hadn't told George yet, but he'd already put both of their lives in danger.

In retrospect, that first moment foreshadowed the rest of their marriage.

"Once I told him I was pregnant everything seemed to change. We seemed to live in a bubble. He didn't raise his hand to strike me in violence. He was kind and loving. It was almost like he was a different person. However, I knew the truth. I knew the kind of life he'd lived as a child…the abuse he'd suffered in the house he'd grown up in. But deep down I just knew he was going to be different. I just *knew* he wasn't going to turn into the man his father was…But before my eyes he slowly became a stranger and I started walking on eggshells."

Miranda took a moment to compose herself and the Asian woman next to her handed her Kleenex.

"The next time he hit me, Piper was three weeks old. She wouldn't stop crying. I fed her, I changed her, I rocked her, but I couldn't figure out what was wrong. George had to get up early to head to work and needed some sleep. I told him I couldn't get the baby quiet, and he slapped me." She shook her head. "He explained that I'd mouthed off to him…but I hadn't. I-I was simply explaining what was going on." Over and over she recounted stories of abuse to the ladies in the room until tears flowed freely.

Their entire marriage had been a cycle of abuse-forgiveness-and-repeat.

"But not anymore," Miranda said. She held her head up high now because she knew the truth. "He's *gone* now. He can't hurt me or my baby anymore."

Miranda blinked, and an image of that fateful night appeared in her mind. She'd aimed that gun at George and had fired a shot into his temple. He wasn't ever going to hurt her or their child again…

"Do you know where he is?" asked a woman across the room. Miranda looked at the woman and realized she currently had a black eye. Miranda knew from when the woman was telling her story that her name was Shelly and she'd left her abuser only two nights ago.

Miranda shook her head and fell back into the lie she'd constructed. "I don't know where George is," she lied. "And I hope he stays gone."

"Your relationship was purposeful," the African American woman—Ms. Pam—said. Miranda slowly moved back to her seat and sat. Ms. Pam looked around the room and locked eyes with each woman. "No matter how horrible the relationship, you have to ask yourself if it taught you something. Did it teach you something?"

A woman nodded and placed a hand over her mouth as if to stifle her groan. Ms. Pam's words had struck a chord.

Ms. Pam continued to look around the room. "Did you learn from the relationship?"

"I learned that I'm stronger than I thought I was," said one woman and another agreed with her.

The women went around the circle and each shared what they'd learned, empowering the next moment.

The circle stopped at Shelly, who shook her head and cried. "I learned that it only takes *one* time for me to leave."

"I learned that I don't want my *next* to pay for the mistakes of my *ex*," said the Asian woman at Miranda's side. The women clapped in agreement, but one sat silently: Miranda.

She hadn't clapped. All that pain that George had put her through had turned into something else: rage. It slowly began to heat her body.

She wasn't a victim anymore. She'd taken her power back from the man that had robbed her of it for all those years.

George was gone…and he wasn't coming back.

"Miranda?" called Ms. Pam.

Miranda looked at her and knew that her face had betrayed her. She sat up in her chair, uncrossed her arms, and took a deep breath. "I learned that men are evil; they're snakes. They can't be trusted to love us. I'm upset and—"

"It's okay to be angry," Ms. Pam said, cutting her off. "But you have to find an outlet for that anger. You can't let it fester, Miranda. You have to let it go or it's going to deprive you of your life changing future."

Miranda shook her head. "I disagree. I think I need to be angry right now. I think I need to feel this and stay in this moment. It's not going to happen again."

"It won't happen again," said Shelly, looking at Miranda through her swollen eye. "We're not the same person we were…at least I'm not. No man is ever going to put his hands on me again." Then, Shelly looked at Ms. Pam. "I just don't know how to move forward."

And Miranda agreed with Shelly. She felt the ice around her heart began to thaw, but she needed to hold onto the ice desperately. She couldn't let her anger go, could she?

She didn't know how to move forward, either. What was she going to do with all this pent-up anger? Her child didn't need the anger. *She* didn't need the anger, but she didn't know what to do with it.

"You can't love on an empty tank," Ms. Pam told the ladies. "You have to find a way to fill yourself back up. Maybe you'll meet someone new, or maybe you won't ever love again…The choice is yours." She held a hand up. "But it *is* up to **you** to find your happiness again. That man may have taken it away from you…but you can get it back. You have to find a way to love yourself *through* the brokenness. It is up to you to embark on your journey to freedom."

Chapter 2

࣓࣓࣓࣓࣓࣓࣓࣓࣓ࣿࣿࣿࣿࣿࣿࣿࣿࣿ

Rachel Richards lay in her king-sized bed, tear stains on her reddened face. She held a balled up piece of tissue in her left hand. At her side, her best friend and neighbor—Freya Goodchild— stroked her frizzy hair.

Freya was dressed in all black and her growing honey blonde hair was piled atop her head in a bun. She caressed Rachel's red hair and tried to wipe her friend's eyes. As she wiped Rachel's eyes, Freya was struck by the contrast in their skin tones. Where she was caramel skinned, her dear friend was pale with skin the color of snow.

"I know, Rae. I know," said Freya, her voice motherly as she tried to coax Rachel out of bed. Today was Jack Richard's funeral and Rachel had refused to get out of bed.

Rachel held a picture of herself and Jack on their wedding day in her right hand. "Oh *Jack!*" she wailed.

"Rachel, you can't be late to your own husband's funeral," Freya told her, her voice soft. "We have to get you ready."

"I can't do this, Freya! I just can't!" She looked at her friend. "How would you feel if Aaron died?"

Freya bit her lip. Her own husband had tricked her and had gotten her pregnant, yet again. That should've been impossible. He was supposed to have undertaken a vasectomy years ago. She now knew that not only had her husband lied about having a vasectomy, but he'd also never scheduled to have one either—she'd checked.

Right about now, she didn't care if Aaron was dead or alive, but she couldn't tell her friend that... not today.

"Honey," Freya finally said, "I'm sorry that you have to do this, but it's the hand you've been dealt."

"It's only been a few days since he died, Freya! Th-The media is going to be there! Paparazzi are going to be circling like vultures trying to get pictures. I can't do this."

"Don't worry about that today," said another voice.

Both women turned and found Rain Fres, another neighbor and dear friend, standing in the doorway. She was dressed in a black dress that complimented her milk chocolate skin.

Rain moved into the room, standing on three-inch Steve Madden heels. Her hair was pulled into a bun atop her head—similar to Freya's style—and she wore red lipstick. "I came to fetch you both," she said, her British accent still thick after all these years in the States. She glanced at Freya. "I figured you'd need some help getting her up today."

Freya nodded and suddenly felt nauseous. She'd been suffering from morning sickness but hadn't yet revealed to her friends that she was pregnant.

She excused herself from the room and headed to the bathroom on the first floor to vomit.

Rain moved to Rachel's bed and sat next to her. "Honey, you have to get up."

"I need more time," Rachel said, sitting up. She brushed her red hair away from her face and looked at Rain through her tears. "How'd you survive when your parents died?"

Rain swallowed hard. She'd lost her parents in a tragic car accident years ago. Sometimes the grief still suffocated her. "I just have to push through, even now," she admitted. "You have to be honest with yourself, Rae. The pain is going to be with you awhile, but you can't let that stop you." She reached out and touched Rachel's chin—lifting it up until their eyes met. "You have to get up, Rachel. You have to do this for Jack. You can fall apart at the funeral, but you have to get up and get there first."

"We'll be at your side the entire time," Freya said as she moved back into the room, a hand pressed to her stomach.

Rain eyed her and raised an eyebrow. "Are you alright?"

Freya dropped her hand. "Yeah, my stomach is just upset. I guess I had some bad pasta last night."

Rachel sniffled and threw the covers back. Rain rose off the bed. "Freya, will you do me a favor?"

"Anything," Freya replied, moving closer.

"Will you help me with my hair?" Rachel tried to smile but only managed a grin.

The organist played a somber tune as the reverend led Rachel and her in-laws—Peter and Janice Richards—into the sanctuary of a catholic church. Rachel wondered where Jack's favorite brother, Jason, was. She hadn't been able to get in touch with him. His other brothers were present though.

Freya walked at her friend's side and Rachel gripped her hand as she caught sight of the open casket.

Rachel wore a simple black dress and a lace veil. Her own mother had commented that the veil was too much, but it wasn't her decision. That was part of why Rachel had requested Freya to walk her down the aisle and not her mother. Regina Adams and her husband, Mark, moved behind their daughter.

The end of the aisle came and now she stood before her husband's casket. She looked down and saw a stranger. Jack's body had been ravaged by his illness and in the end he was a shell of his former self.

His face was sunken and his hair thin. His jaundiced skin was now pale. She barely recognized him.

As she leaned down to kiss his cold cheek, a tear fell onto his face. Rachel kissed his cheek and stood up, wiping the tear off his face with her gloved hand.

Freya led her to the pew and sat Rachel down beside her in-laws and then sat next to her. She looked over her shoulder and caught sight of her husband and their five children. Surprisingly, her children were silent and well behaved. Her son, Aaron Junior, waved at her. She smiled and waved back. Then, she caught her husband's eye and wiped the smile off her face. Aaron Senior waved at her, but she glared and turned around.

He frowned in confusion but quickly composed himself. Freya had forced him out of their marital bed days ago and he didn't know why. She wasn't ready to tell him what he'd done to her. She wasn't ready to admit to anyone that she was pregnant. She hadn't even decided if she was going to keep the baby.

What was she going to do with a sixth child?! Freya sighed and shook her head. Now wasn't the time to think about her problems. Today was about Rachel. Today was about Jack.

She looked at the casket and wondered how she'd feel if it was Aaron in the casket. Would she grieve her husband of ten years?

Rachel wiped her tears with a handkerchief and looked at the reverend. He nodded and began the service.

Five rows behind Jack's family, Miranda and her daughter, Piper, sat with Rain and Prudence. Rachel's friends had her back. Only Miranda hadn't stuck to the traditional black dress code for the funeral. She wore a plum colored swing dress with a stylish bow.

The only people missing were Prue's husband—Donatello— and Miranda's husband. Derrick Fres, Rain's husband, sat across the church with Aaron Senior and his children.

Rachel's mind raced with thoughts of her union to Jack. They'd been married for twelve years and had been through so much together. She tried to focus on the reverend's words but kept getting distracted by the corpse before her.

She wished someone had closed the casket.

The reverend raised his hands towards the congregation. "So, as we mourn the passing of Jack, we give thanks to God, for we do not grieve as those who have no hope, but as those who place their trust in the one true God." The organist struck up another somber tune and the reverend gestured for the congregation to rise.

Had the funeral ended already? Rachel rose but didn't recall a single word spoken by the reverend.

Four of Jack's teammates approached the coffin and the funeral director finally closed the casket. Rachel sighed in relief.

She eyed the football players. She wondered if Jack had done drugs with any of them. None of them had visited him in the hospital. Were they even his friends?

He'd contracted Hepatitis C after doing drugs with some teammates. Jack Richards had lived a wild life filled with friends and whores, but in the end, it was only his wife who'd been at his side.

Jack had suffered in the end. His organs had begun to shut down and as a result of complications with his disease, he'd lost his life.

The funeral director led the four football players, who'd stuffed their buff bodies into suits, down the aisle; then the reverend motioned for Rachel and the other members of the family to follow.

Freya reached for Rachel's hand, but Rachel shook her head. "I'm fine now," Rachel whispered. "It's over." She had to admit she felt better now.

It was real to her now. She'd seen Jack's lifeless body. They'd closed the casket. She was a widow now.

Now, she just needed to get through the burial and she could begin to put all of this behind her.

Rachel neared the exit and something caught her eye. Near the double doors that would lead outside and off to the side among the crowd stood an unfamiliar face. Was she a reporter who'd snuck into the funeral?

The woman's skin was tanned, and her brown hair was tousled and shoulder length. She looked to be Hispanic, but Rachel wasn't sure. Something about her was familiar, but Rachel couldn't place her.

The woman wore a leopard print dress that Rachel thought was tacky, but that wasn't the only thing that had caught Rachel's eye.

As Rachel passed the last few rows she noticed that the woman was holding the hand of a little girl. The little girl wore a black dress and Mary Jane shoes.

The little girl looked up and met Rachel's gaze. All of the air left Rachel's lungs and she gasped. She grabbed Freya's hand, startling the woman.

"What is it, Rae?" Freya asked, forcing her friend to keep her legs moving.

"Those eyes," Rachel whispered, and Freya looked around, confused.

"Whose eyes?" Freya asked, looking in the audience.

Rachel couldn't take her eyes off the little girl. Those eyes…such *familiar* eyes.

Rachel could barely walk. Her knees shook and she suddenly felt weak. She leaned into Freya and her eyes grew watery.

Those eyes, she thought. *Those familiar eyes!*

Chapter 3

⌘⌘⌘⌘⌘⌘⌘⌘⌘⌘

The night of the funeral Rain and Derrick Fres walked into their half-empty colonial home and Rain locked the door. Less than four days ago, her husband had informed her that he'd been offered a new position at Star Best Music Group in New York City and they'd be relocating.

They'd been packing for days and she'd yet to announce the move to her dear friends. So much had happened in such a short time. Rachel's husband had died and everything had been turned upside down.

Movers had already removed their living and dining room furniture and sent it to their new place and had also taken Derrick's studio apart and shipped that, too.

Rain and her husband had been living in a limbo of sorts lately.

Derrick had seemed detached and distant and she'd responded in kind.

However, after watching Rachel at the funeral today Rain had come to realize that life was too short.

She moved towards her husband and wrapped her arms around him from behind. Derrick turned and kissed her. The first kiss was gentle.

"Are you alright?" Derrick asked, his strong arms wrapped around his wife of nearly two years.

She shook her head. "Not at all. I don't ever want to end up like Rachel…She's a widow…and still so young." She exhaled.

"Well, one day that's going to happen," Derrick responded. "We all have to die, Rain."

"Maybe we'll go together," she told him. "Maybe I won't have to be a widow at all."

"Don't worry about that right now. We're going to be old people when we die. You're not going to lose me anytime soon."

Rain kissed her husband and soaked in his scent. He wore a classic cologne that drove Rain wild. Derrick moved his lips over hers and she responded with an open mouth.

Without warning, Derrick stopped kissing her and just looked directly into her eyes.

"What's the matter?" Rain asked.

"Nothing," he responded. "I just wanted to look at you for a moment." He took a step back and admired her curvy figure. She was so beautiful. "There's so much about you that I still don't know."

"I can say the same. We've been together for what seems like ages, but I still have so many questions."

"Can we talk for a minute?" he asked, and she grinned. In that moment, Derrick knew they would be alright. Rain would do whatever it took to please him. He loved how submissive she was becoming.

"I'd like that a lot," she replied. She turned around so he could unzip her dress and then moved to their bedroom. Derrick moved to the master bedroom and watched as his wife slipped under the covers of their bed. "Let's just lie here and talk."

Derrick removed his pants and shirt, revealing a t-shirt and boxers.

He smiled. "I'm down for that. I could just look into those beautiful eyes of yours for the rest of my life."

"You're just saying that so you can get inside my pants," she said, laughing.

"You aren't wearing any," he told her, climbing into bed. "Maybe if I look in your eyes long enough, I'll discover what's going on behind them."

She shook her head, loosening her growing hair from its bun. "I doubt it."

"And why is that, Mrs. Fres?"

"Probably because I'm falling asleep."

Derrick frowned. "I thought you wanted to talk?"

She yawned and leaned her head against her husband's shoulder. He wrapped his arms around her and his face drooped in disappointment. "Good night, husband."

He couldn't believe that she was about to fall asleep on him. Every time he thought they were getting closer, she'd just pull away from him. He rolled his eyes and wondered why he even bothered.

Minutes later, he looked down at Rain's face and realized she had fallen asleep. Derrick moved her head away from his chest and to a pillow and then climbed out of bed.

He headed downstairs and checked to make sure the door was locked; sometimes his wife didn't turn the latch all the way. After doing that, he moved to the window and gazed out into the street.

All of Lyfe Road seemed to be asleep. He glanced at Prudence and Donatello's house. The lights were off. Perhaps they were both asleep, too.

He would definitely have to talk to his neighbor before he and Rain left for New York. He and Donatello had unfinished business…

Derrick moved back upstairs and found his wife sleeping as though she didn't have a care in the world. She perplexed him. Maybe he'd never figure her out.

But why bother? He now worked as a music producer for Star BMG. During his last trip to the label, many women had thrown themselves at him with hopes of becoming a star. So many women had offered him sexual favors in exchange for time in the studio with his beats. Perhaps he didn't need to focus on Rain as much anymore.

If she didn't want to fully commit to their marriage then why should he? He enjoyed her company and when they had sex it was great, but something was missing.

Perhaps he needed to focus on his wants and needs for a while.

Derrick laid down and as he found his sleeping position, Rain rolled over and wrapped her arm around him.

He pushed her arm off him. Sometimes she craved intimacy and other times she rejected it. Derrick didn't have time for her games. There were other fish in the sea…

The next morning a ringing phone awakened Derrick and he hurried to pick up his cellphone before the noise woke Rain.

He glanced at the clock on the nightstand and it read 6:03a.m. Climbing out of bed, Derrick moved towards the hallway and answered the phone. He rubbed the sleep from his eyes.

"Hello?"

"We need to talk," came the voice on the other end.

Derrick immediately recognized the deep voice. "Donatello, hi. Why are you calling so early?"

"We need to talk. Meet me out front in twenty minutes." And with that, the call ended.

"Everything okay?" came a voice from behind Derrick. He jumped and found his wife standing in the doorway that led to their master bedroom.

"Yeah, everything's okay. Go back to bed."

She ignored him and walked towards him. "Who was that? Was it your mom? She's normally the only one who calls this early in the morning."

"Bill collector," Derrick lied. He moved past his wife and headed to the master bathroom to brush his teeth. "I'm going to go grab us some breakfast. What would you like?"

"I'm not hungry," Rain replied. "I'm going to go into the office and turn in my notice."

Derrick nodded and rushed out of the bathroom, pulling on sweats as he moved past his wife. "That's good. You've been wasting your time as a real estate agent any way."

Rain stopped and looked at him. She started to speak then thought better of it. In the next moment Derrick was out the door before Rain could mutter an "I love you."

Derrick met Donatello Cameron on the curb in front of his house. Donatello sat in the back of a black Lincoln town car driven by one of his goons.

Derrick and Donatello had a long history, but Derrick hoped they'd be able to end that history on a good note.

"Donatello, I—"

"Before you open your mouth to lie, remember that I probably already know the truth." Donatello looked at his neighbor and glared. "You've been a very naughty boy, Derrick Fres."

Derrick's jaw clenched. He hated being called a boy, especially since he was a black man. He was far from a boy. He was a grown man and even though he'd borrowed hundreds of thousands of dollars from the loan shark that now sat next to him, that didn't mean that he should be belittled. He'd done so many things in Donatello's name…so many *horrible* things. But that needed to end today.

"I was going to tell you, Donny. I just needed more time."

"I want my money *before* you leave for New York," Donatello told him. "I want it all…in *full*."

Derrick's eyes widened. "Are you serious?! You've got to be kidding me! When I shot Miranda in the hospital you told me that would wipe my debt! You told me that—"

"I told you if you **killed** her that I'd wipe your debt," Donatello corrected. "She didn't die, Derrick."

"That's not my fault! I shot her point blank! You can't go back on your word—"

"I want the money in cash," Donatello said, ignoring him.

Derrick nodded. "Alright." He shut his mouth for a moment. Things were getting out of hand. *I might as well get this over with.* "I'll have the money tomorrow. But after I pay you back, that's *it*, Donatello. I want to be set free; no more forcing me to do your dirty work." *He's truly a monster,* Derrick thought. *He doesn't have a heart.*

Donatello held a hand up. "I'm a man of my word. Once you pay me my money back, I'll wipe the slate clean."

"Thank you, Donatello! I—"

Donatello raised a hand to silence him. "You have a clean slate with *me*, but Miranda is another matter altogether."

Derrick's expression darkened and he looked away.

Rain looked out the window. Derrick had lied to her again. He'd told her he was going to grab them breakfast, but instead he'd climbed in a car with Donatello and was still sitting out front.

Who did he think she was, Boo-Boo the Fool?!

Rain grew irritated and turned to finish packing the house. She heaved a box into the living room. Sweat trickled down her forehead. Here she was, uprooting her life and quitting her job to join the man she'd tied her life to and he couldn't even be honest with her.

Why were they married if they couldn't be honest with each other?

Suddenly, the front door opened and Derrick appeared in the hallway a few moments later. "Where's breakfast?" she asked, grinning at him as if oblivious to the fact that he'd never gone anywhere.

"They were out of bagels," he lied. Rain's smile melted off her face. She turned away and busied herself with packing a box.

"So, how's the packing going?"

"Pretty good, I guess. Half of the house is ready to go." Rain couldn't understand why he lied about the simple things. If he lied about the simple things, then what else was he lying about?

Derrick pulled the box from his wife's hands and placed it in a stack alongside the wall near the front door. "Have you told your friends you're moving to New York?"

Rain turned to look at him. *Have you told me why you're constantly lying and hanging with Donatello?* But she knew she'd never outright ask him that. Instead, she shook her head. "No, I haven't been able to find the right time."

Derrick rolled his eyes and walked away.

"Derrick!" Rain called after him. Her husband moved into the next room and Rain followed him.

"You've been complaining about the move and how this is going to affect your *'sisters',* but you've yet to tell them. Pretty soon it's going to be too late."

"With Jack dying, it just didn't seem to be the right time to break the news to them."

"Rain, we're leaving Lyfe Road in three days! The band's going to break up either way. It's best to rip the band aid off now then to wait until the last minute."

She nodded. "I'll tell them today."

Rain called her friends and they agreed to meet her over Rachel's. Rachel had chimed in that she could use the company.

Rain paced the floor as the five women gathered in Rachel's living room.

Rachel wore pajamas and looked a mess, but she was allowed. At least she'd gotten out of bed today.

Miranda sat in the corner of the living room, her eyes watching Rain as she paced nervously. "What's wrong, Rain?" she asked. "Whatever it is, just tell us. This pacing back and forth is giving me anxiety."

Rain froze and faced the group. Prudence sat up straight and waited for Rain to talk. Freya appeared to be in another place even though she sat next to Miranda. Rain decided she'd have to ask her if she were alright after all of this was over.

"I probably should've told you all days ago, but I have to tell you something. It's about me and Derrick."

Prue looked up. "You're getting a divorce? Good for you, Rain! You could do so much better."

Freya gasped and looked at Prue as Rain's face shifted to an expression of shock.

"Prue!" exclaimed Miranda.

Prue shrugged. "I mean, it's okay if you're getting a divorce, Rain. No one's going to judge you. I mean, Donny and I...well we're probably getting a divorce, too, so I understand."

"Prue..." said Rachel, a warning in her voice.

But that didn't stop Prue. She kept rambling on. "I don't blame him though. I mean, I cheated on him and—"

Freya gasped. "You *cheated* on Donatello? Prue—"

"Ladies," Rain called, getting their attention. She sighed. "Derrick and I aren't getting a divorce." She frowned. "Prue, why would you say something like that?"

Prue looked embarrassed and dropped her gaze. "Sorry...I guess I shouldn't have assumed."

Rain exhaled and shook her head.

"Then what is it?" Rachel asked. She looked exhausted and like she needed to get back in bed but was fighting to remain present.

"Derrick was offered a position at Star BMG, and he accepted."

The ladies beamed and clapped and congratulated her...everyone but Rachel. Rachel didn't divert her gaze from Rain, nor was she smiling.

"But?" said Rachel and the room filled with silence as the others looked from Rachel to Rain. "I sense a '*but*' coming, Rain."

Rain sighed and brushed her hands together. "The job's in New York."

The room grew eerily silent as the words settled in. Rain had expected the women to be shocked, but not silent. "Not all of you speak at once," she told them as she crossed her arms over her chest.

Freya shifted in her seat and cleared her throat. "Wow, Rain…so you'll be moving?"

Rain tucked a strand of brown hair behind her ear and then nodded. "We're leaving in a few days."

Prue sucked in a breath and covered her mouth.

Rachel rose to her feet and every pair of eyes shifted to look at her. "I can't handle this right now." She shook her head. "Congratulations, Rain." And with that, Rachel turned and headed upstairs to her room.

"Rae," Rain called after her, but the woman was gone. She felt her heart twist in pain. That hurt more than she'd realize it would.

"Why'd you wait to tell us?" Miranda asked.

"Jack had just died, but—"

"His death had nothing to do with the rest of us," Prudence said, lowering her voice to respect Rachel.

"She's right," agreed Freya. "You could've told us." Rain dropped her head in shame. She'd let her girls down. "Unbow your head, sista."

Rain looked up and saw Freya gesture with her own chin what to do. As two of the few black women on Lyfe Road, Freya and Rain had a special bond. The color divide between dark and light skinned black women that often hindered some women hadn't stopped them from being good friends, nor had it been a problem for them. That wasn't always the case in the African American community.

Freya and Rain both believed that they were equals. Even though they'd both been raised to believe that being light skinned was better than dark skinned, Freya never acted on it. That was utter foolishness. She loved Rain all the same just for being a genuine friend.

"You have nothing to feel guilty about," Freya reassured her. "You married the man you love. Where he goes, you go."

"And had we known ahead of time, Rachel probably would've baked you some going away cookies," Miranda added, trying to lighten the mood.

The others smiled but the gesture didn't reach their eyes. They were losing one of the members of their sisterhood.

"Perhaps I should go check on Rachel," Freya said.

"Let me do it," Rain told her. Freya nodded and Rain moved to the stairs.

On the second floor, Rain knocked on the closed door and didn't wait for an answer. She opened the door and found Rachel in bed balled into a fetal position.

"Rachel," Rain called.

"Come in," Rachel told her. Rain moved across the room and took a seat on the bed. "I'm not upset." She turned over and faced Rain. "My behavior has nothing to do with you. I'm just…I'm just spoiled, I guess. I just don't understand."

"What don't you understand?" Rain asked, her tone gentle.

"I just don't understand why everyone leaves." Tears fell from her eyes and Rain pulled Rachel into her arms, hugging her.

"Rachel, I'll only be a plane ride away. I'm not gone forever. You're still my friend. You know that."

"But—"

Rain shushed her and pulled out of their embrace so she could look the woman in the eye. "Regardless of where I live we will always be friends. Regardless of what happens in life, regardless of how troubled or *restless* we may get, I will *always* be here for you. You aren't alone, Rachel."

Rachel sniffled and nodded. "I'm such a mess." She laughed and Rain laughed, too. "Can I ask you a question?"

Rachel eyed her friend and Rain nodded.

"Is this what you want? Is this *truly* what you want? Do you want to go to New York?"

Rain sat there for a moment and then opened her mouth to speak. She moved her lips, but nothing came out.

"You don't have to answer," Rachel told her. "I'm only asking because I just want you to make sure that this is what you want, too. You're uprooting your life for this man. Just make sure that it's worth it. You matter, too, Rain."

"I love him," Rain told her friend, but Rachel wasn't convinced.

For that matter, Rain wasn't sure she was convinced either. She had her doubts about her union with Derrick.

Had they gotten married too soon?

There was so much that they still didn't know about each other. Sometimes Derrick scared her. Sometimes it was like she was looking at a stranger.

Rachel reached out and took her friend's hand. "You're important to me, Rain. I just want you to be okay. If you start sacrificing now and you don't stick up for yourself, he'll keep taking from you and chipping little bits of you away. One day, you'll wake up and realize that you've lived *his* life…and not yours…Trust me, I'm speaking from experience. I spent our entire marriage devoted to Jack and I have nothing to show for it. No education…no children…no accomplishments of my own."

"But you've done great things, Rae!" said Rain. "This is your grief talking!"

"Is it?" asked Rachel. She shook her head. "Look at me, Rain. Who am I?"

"You're my dear friend," the woman replied.

"Beyond that? I only have my high school diploma. I dropped out of college shortly after Jack and I started dating. I don't have anything of my own! I have **his money** now. I live in *his* house! When you and the girls leave tonight, this home will go back to being just another house."

"Don't be so hard on yourself, Rachel."

She shook her head. "It's always been too silent here, even when Jack was alive. And now that he's gone, I'm beginning to loathe the silence…it's a constant silence that never lets up." Rachel gripped her friend's hand. "Rain, love yourself *first*. Don't end up like me."

Thunder sounded outside the window and the two ladies realized it was starting to rain.

Downstairs, Miranda pulled on her jacket and headed out into the rain. She eyed Rain's home and caught sight of Derrick's car in the driveway.

Without a thought, she headed towards the house.

Chapter 4

❧ ❧ ❧ ❧ ❧ ❧ ❧ ❧ ❧

Derrick stood in front of the floor length window of his living room watching the rain fall. He sipped on vodka from a glass and his thoughts turned to the darkest deed he couldn't wait to leave behind…

Derrick walked down the hall of the hospital, searching for room 427. He wore a black shirt and matching slacks. In his hand was a brown paper bag.

He picked up his pace and made his way to Miranda's room. Finally, he found the room and opened the door.

As he entered the hospital room, he placed the paper bag on the tray in the room.

Derrick looked at Miranda. He knew she was in a coma, but it simply looked as though she were resting.

He opened the paper bag and reached inside it, pulling out a silver pistol. He pulled out a silencer and attached it to the tip.

Swallowing hard, Derrick slowly aimed the weapon at Miranda. He couldn't believe Donatello had put him up to this. He hated being in debt to that man.

His stomach churned. He couldn't believe he was about to end an innocent woman's life to wipe out his debt.

"This won't be bloody at all, I promise," he whispered as he aimed the gun at Miranda's chest—which rose and fell as she breathed. "Don't let this bullet in your pretty little chest give you a fright."

Slowly, but surely, Miranda's eyes fluttered open. And at that **exact** moment, Derrick Fres pulled the trigger.

The bullet slammed into Miranda's chest and she groaned. Her eyes fluttered and opened wide.

Derrick gasped and took a step back, shaking his head. Her eyes were open!

"You're awake!" he exclaimed, his heart racing. "No, no, no, no!"

He watched as a bit of blood began to stain her hospital gown. Perhaps the bullet had struck her heart and she was slowly dying.

Her eyes stared straight ahead—stared at him. But she couldn't see him, could she? She didn't appear to be conscious.

He'd shot her point blank and she wasn't going to survive this. She couldn't!

Derrick quickly placed the pistol in the brown bag and rushed out of the hospital room.

Miranda Copeland was going to die.

No, she was dead! Right? He'd shot her. He hadn't missed his mark.

His debt would be wiped clean with Donatello. He and Rain would be free. When Miranda died, George Copeland would receive a life insurance check and in turn would be able to pay the money he owed Donatello back, as well, plus interest.

It had all worked out seamlessly, right?

Derrick jumped as the sound of the pistol firing echoed in his mind. He shook the memory off and turned away from the floor length mirror.

As he turned to leave the room he jumped and dropped his glass. The glass shattered as it hit the floor, spilling vodka onto the wooden floor.

Before him stood the woman from his nightmares.

"Miranda!" he exclaimed.

How'd she get into the house? Had Rain given her a key or something?

Miranda moved from the shadows of the hallway and into the living room. She stopped about six feet away from Derrick and glared up at him—he was taller than she was.

Derrick gulped and took in Miranda's appearance. She wasn't some timid woman anymore. She looked hard and cold...she looked like a killer now.

He wondered what had brought about this metamorphosis.

"What are you doing here?" he asked her, subconsciously backing away from her.

"What's wrong, Derrick?" she asked, a smirk on her face. He shook his head and she took a step forward. "I've come to recall a day when a man in all black entered my hospital room and aimed a pistol at me."

Derrick gulped and Miranda stepped closer to him. He backed into a chair and began to circle the living room. "Miranda...wait."

Her eyes seemed to burrow into his soul and Derrick couldn't take it. His heart raced and he felt sweat break out on his forehead.

"I *saw* you, Derrick. I saw *you*."

"How can you be so sure—"

She held up a hand to silence him. "Don't even try to deny it, Derrick. You and I both know it was you. You're the one who shot me that day."

Derrick looked at her side and realized that she held a gun in her hand. Miranda caught sight of where his eyes were looking, and she raised the gun. "You see this?"

"What are you going to do with that?" he asked, fear filling his voice.

"Don't worry, Derrick. I wouldn't dare hurt Rain that way. For some reason, she loves you."

"Then what do you plan to do with it?"

She shrugged. "I brought the gun in case you decided to try to finish me off."

He shook his head. "You have to understand. I never wanted to kill you! I have PTSD now because of it! Donatello made me do it and—"

"What is it with you men and Donatello Cameron?" She shook her head, utterly disgusted. "You're all fools if you're in league with him."

Derrick slowly began to raise his arms in mock surrender. "I'm sorry, Miranda…I really am."

"Save your apologies for someone who wants them." She turned and headed towards the front door. She opened it and the sound of rain filled the quiet house. "But mark my words, Derrick Fres, you'll receive yours in due time. There's a special place in Hell for people like you."

"Please don't tell Rain."

Miranda looked over her shoulder and her face twisted in disbelief. "After all you've done, that's what you're worried about?" She stood in the doorway as thunder sounded and the rain continued to pour.

"I can't lose her," he told her.

Miranda was taken aback by his words. "You say you can't bear to lose her, but you were more than willing to take me from my little girl…" She pursed her lips in frustration. "Fuck you, Derrick."

And with that, she left the house, slamming the door behind her.

Derrick felt his racing heart suddenly sink. He looked at his feet and realized there was a puddle near his shoes.

He'd wet his pants.

Chapter 5

Freya Goodchild pulled her minivan into a parking spot and shifted the gear into park. She turned the minivan off, removed her keys from the ignition, took a deep breath, and patted her pudgy stomach.

"Well, it's time to see what we're dealing with." She unlocked the vehicle and climbed out. She pulled a jean jacket over her caramel skin and then headed into her doctor's office.

Twenty-two minutes later, Freya lay on an examination table with a sonographer conducting the sonogram. Freya placed a hand on her forehead and exhaled. She was nervous.

She'd never had a transvaginal ultrasound before. Even with five pregnancies under her belt she still was experiencing new things.

Her mouth felt dry and she could feel a film of sweat collecting on her brow.

"It's okay, Miss," the woman performing her sonogram said. "Relax." Freya smiled politely. In the next moment, the woman shifted the screen and stroked a few keys on her keyboard. "Alright, look at the screen"—she gestured to a speck on the screen—"*here.*"

Freya followed the woman's hand as she pointed. The image on the screen was about the size of a blueberry.

"This little spec is your growing little bundle of joy," the woman told her.

After giving birth to five children, Freya knew exactly where to look before the woman had even pointed.

"My *baby*," she said, a lump rising in her throat.

How could she ever have considered having an abortion? She'd struggled through five pregnancies and had survived. She was raising five healthy children and surviving…she could do it once more.

It wasn't the child's fault that it had been conceived.

The technician cocked her head and frowned. "Wait a minute."

"What?" asked Freya, eyeing the screen. "What do you see? Is something wrong?"

Freya knew from experience that sonographers were NOT supposed to react during an ultrasound. That meant something was—

Could the technician detect signs of a possible miscarriage? Was something wrong with her baby?

"There's nothing wrong, Mrs. Goodchild. I'm sorry to have alarmed you."

Freya relaxed. "Then what is it?" *She must be new,* Freya thought to herself.

"Look here," the woman told her, pointing at the screen again. Freya quickly obeyed, but all she saw was the same image. "This is your baby."

Freya nodded and tried to keep her eyes from rolling. Clearly this woman was fresh out of trade school. Why was she repeating herself? "Yes, you just showed me that," Freya told her in a condescending tone.

The woman smiled politely and moved the wand inside of Freya. "And *this* is your baby."

Freya's heart froze. She now saw not one, but *two* gestational sacs on the ultrasound. Freya sat up on her elbows and looked at the frozen image on the screen. *"Twins?!"*

Not one, but *two* new mouths to feed! *SEVEN* children!

Freya suddenly felt light headed. She leaned back against the examination table and took a deep breath.

"I'd say you're about seven weeks pregnant, Mrs. Goodchild."

She was seven weeks pregnant with her sixth and seventh child.

Everything was about to change. Nothing would ever be the same.

Freya felt pressure in her nether regions and the transducer was pulled out of her.

Suddenly, Freya burst into tears—overcome with emotions.

The sonographer looked at her, frowned, and rose to her feet. "I-I'll give you a moment." And with that, the woman left the room, closing the door behind her.

Freya looked at the screen through her tears and cried even harder.

"What am I going to do with *seven* kids?"

March 22, 2007

Freya came running down the stairs dressed in a pantsuit. Her golden-brown hair was curled and spilled over her shoulders. She moved into the kitchen where Aaron Senior and their eldest daughter—Francesca—made breakfast together.

She didn't have time to think. She didn't have time to worry about the secret she'd been hiding. She just simply didn't have time.

Ever since she'd kicked him out of their marital bed without a word, he'd been making an effort to not only help around the house, but also to spend more time with the kids.

"Hey, you," he said, grinning at his wife. "What's the special occasion?"

"I have a job interview," she replied, kissing her daughter atop the head. She avoided eye contact with the man she'd tied her life to through marriage.

Aaron's jaw dropped. "Wh-What? You're going back to work?"

Freya grabbed a piece of toast and spread some butter on it. She threw her hair over her shoulder and eyed her husband. "What, you didn't expect this black woman to stay home forever raising your kids did you? You thought I was just some lazy heifer, huh?"

He looked taken aback. "Freya, what's gotten into you?" He moved across the kitchen, but Freya moved away from him. "Why are you bringing race into this?"

"You didn't want me to work, Aaron, remember? When I got pregnant with Francesca you asked me to stay home and—"

"Perhaps we shouldn't have this conversation right now?" He nodded at their child, who was still helping with breakfast.

Freya sighed. "Fran, go help your sisters get dressed."

"Okay, mommy," the child replied.

As their eldest child headed up the stairs, Freya turned to her husband. "Aaron, I'm going back to work. I'm not asking your permission."

"What's gotten into you lately?" He moved closer to her. "I thought we were doing better. We were finally having sex again, we were communicating, and I was doing better with the kids."

She looked at him. "I didn't know I needed a reason to want to get back out there and start working again. I didn't know I needed you to approve my choices." She crossed her arms over her chest. "Do I need to ask you for permission, Aaron? Is that what you want?"

Aaron opened his mouth but nothing came out.

"I didn't know we'd stepped back into slavery, Aaron, where *'Massa'* gets to go to work and his whore stays home and takes care of the children of the plantation."

Aaron's eyes grew wide with shock. "Freya, what the hell is wrong with you?! Have you lost your mind?!"

"I don't need your permission to work! I don't need you to tell me what I can and can't do! I don't need—"

"I never said you couldn't work. I only suggested you should spend more time at home." He shook his head and jabbed a finger in her direction. "No, no, this is something else. Race has never been a problem in our marriage! A-And you've *never* talked to me this way before! I—"

"I'm pregnant," she blurted out.

Aaron blinked and closed his mouth. Shock moved across his face before he took a step back.

They both stood in the kitchen, silent.

"I'm pregnant," she repeated, her voice stronger this time. "I'm pregnant and I ***shouldn't*** be!"

Aaron began to stutter, and Freya simply stood there glaring at him. "Listen, Freya, I—"

"You WHAT, Aaron? You're a selfish bastard, did you know that? I TRUSTED you! The first time you lied we ended up with Anthony! But, no! You said you would finally go and do what you should've done the first time! You said you had the vasectomy yet here we are: PREGNANT!" She shook her head. "Let me correct that. Here *I am: PREGNANT!*" She scoffed. "You don't love me, Aaron…you can't, because if you did, you wouldn't have taken my choices away from me."

He reached out to her, but she smacked his hand away.

"Don't touch me!" she shouted.

Aaron looked around the corner to make sure the children weren't listening, but sure enough, five pairs of eyes were on the stairwell listening. "Freya, let's talk about this later."

"You don't get to decide when we talk about this!" she shouted, tears threatening to spill from her eyes. "I want you out of this house!"

He whirled around, his eyes wide. "Wait a second, Freya, let's talk this through this."

"You're a liar, Aaron Goodchild. You're a liar and you took my choices away from me. You thought you owned me…You thought you owned my body! YOU made this choice and didn't think me worthy of being included."

"I didn't want a vasectomy!" he shouted.

"And I didn't want another baby!" Her chest heaved in and out.

A deep silence filled the air and Melody began to cry. Aaron Junior wrapped his arms around his sister.

Freya dabbed at her eyes so her mascara wouldn't run. She sniffled and threw her hair back—composing herself.

Francesca looked from her father to her mother and then reached for her other sister's hand.

Aubrey looked at her older sister and frowned. If Francesca was worried then she had to worry, too.

"We need to talk through this," Aaron said, lowering his voice.

"The time for talking has passed," she replied. She eyed her children and her chest tightened to see them so distraught.

"Freya, please…"

She tore her eyes from her children and looked at the man who she'd once loved.

"I don't want to be late to this interview," she told him. "I need this job because my family now needs the income."

"Freya, what are you talking about? You don't have to—"

"Oh, yes I do, Aaron! I have to work; I need to work. A single parent can't raise kids without income."

Realization filled Aaron's eyes. "*Single* parent? Freya, you haven't been single in over a decade."

When Freya spoke this time, her voice was even and clear. "Well, guess what, Mr. Big Shot? I've been raising these damn kids all by myself all this time! But you've made the decision to keep it that way." She removed her wedding ring and placed it on the kitchen counter. "Like I said, I want you out of this house. Preferably you'll be out before I get home this evening."

She turned and headed out of the side door, the keys to Aaron's car in her hands. She cranked the engine and pulled out of the driveway.

"What just happened?" Aaron Junior asked his father as he moved into the kitchen.

Aaron Senior just stood there with shock etched on his red face. When their father didn't reply, Aaron Junior turned to his big sister.

"Fran, what just happened?" the boy asked. In that moment, her four siblings looked at her.

Francesca avoided their eyes and looked straight at her dad. He seemed to be staring off into nothingness. Francesca's lower lip began to tremble. "Mom just told dad she wants a divorce."

Chapter 6

❦❦❦❦❦❦❦❦❦❦

Miranda's doorbell rang and she moved through her white colonial house with the blue shutters. She opened the door and found two men standing on her doorstep. She closed her door slightly, using it as a shield between her and the men.

"Yes, can I help you?" she asked, eyeing them suspiciously.

One man reached inside his suit jacket and flashed a badge. "I'm Detective Burns and this is my partner, Detective Matthews."

"What can I do for you?" Miranda eased the door open wider. At least they weren't kidnappers sent by Donatello as retribution for her threatening Derrick. She'd already been kidnapped one too many times for her liking.

"We just wanted to follow up on the missing person's report you filed a few days ago," said the one named Matthews.

"It's about your husband, George, right?" asked the other.

Miranda swallowed the bile that rose in her throat at the mention of the despicable man she'd made the mistake of marrying.

But despite herself, she nodded. "Yes, he's been gone for some time."

Her black eye was still visible even though it was beginning to heal. Detective Burns gestured to her face. "Did he give you that shiner?"

Miranda nodded and self-consciously touched the bruise. "Would you gentlemen like to come in?" She opened the door wider for them and they moved into the house.

Miranda showed them to the living room. "I only have a few minutes," she told them as she took a seat on the couch. "I have to pick my daughter up from school soon."

"We won't hold you long then," said Detective Burns as Detective Matthews pulled out a small notepad.

"When was the last time you saw Mr. Copeland?" asked Detective Matthews.

"It's in the report," Miranda said. She adjusted her sitting position.

Donatello had told her what to do and what to say on that fateful night... She wasn't going to deviate from that story now.

Miranda's thoughts turned to March 18th...

On March 18, 2007, Miranda Copeland took her life back. After suffering years of abuse at his hands, Miranda murdered her husband on that cold, stormy night.

Without warning, George struck her. She aimed the pistol at him and he charged forward. She closed her eyes and pulled the trigger.

Miranda had heard George grunt and when she opened her eyes, he was touching a bloody wound in his chest. He wasn't dead though. He was still moving towards her.

She screamed, as he charged forward, and ducked. George yelled and fell over the second-floor banister and slammed into the floor below.

As Miranda stood up, she caught sight of George's blood pooling around his body.

Suddenly, George began to move.

Miranda ran down the stairs and by the time she reached the living room, George was on his feet.

George took a step and then another one, but Miranda wasn't going to let him put his hands on her ever again. Enough was enough.

She aimed for his temple and pulled the trigger again.

George collapsed—dead.

The moment George's body hit the floor, Miranda exhaled.

It was over.

George was dead.

However, once her actions caught up to her brain, she began to shake. She moved towards the phone and lifted it from its cradle.

She was about to dial a number but hesitated. A fraction of a second later she changed her mind and dialed Donatello.

"He's dead," she said, her voice clear and sure.

On the other end of the phone, Donatello Cameron let out a heavy sigh. Miranda imagined he was massaging his temple in frustration.

"Miranda, what have you done?"

"I ended this. Now, please, Donatello...help me. I'll get the $20,000 he owes you first thing in the morning when the bank opens, but I need your help now. I need you to get rid of his body."

The line clicked and Miranda realized he'd hung up on her. Outside the window thunder sounded and lightning flashed.

What was she going to do if Donatello didn't come through for her? She had to get George's body out of there!

If Donatello didn't help her, she'd just say it was self-defense. And truly, it was! She'd filed police reports in the past and he'd recently been arrested for beating her unconscious.

George was no saint.

Miranda lowered herself to the floor and sobbed.

Suddenly, the doorbell rang. She gasped and looked at the door. The porch light was off and she couldn't tell who it was.

She dropped the gun and forced herself to stand. The doorbell rang again and then someone started beating on the door.

"Miranda, it's me!" came the voice from the porch.

She instantly recognized the voice. Donatello had come after all.

She rushed towards the door and opened it. Before her, drenched from the rain, stood Donatello and two of his goons—the same two men who'd kidnapped her days ago.

She took a step back and let them in the house. Now wasn't the time to let her fear of the events get to her. They had a job to do.

"Oh, Miranda," said Donatello, his voice filled with wonder. From the living room, Miranda could hear the kingpin clapping.

She moved into the living room and glanced down at her husband's corpse.

"Help me, please," she said.

Donatello faced her and then snapped his fingers at his two goons. They instantly turned to face him and seemed to straighten up. Donatello turned his eyes on Miranda and she felt a chill run down her spine. His gaze was piercing. "Do you have any shovels?"

She nodded. "In the shed."

"Get them," he ordered his goons.

The two men lifted George off the floor—one grabbed him under the arms and the other by the ankles. His blood dripped onto the floor.

Miranda moved to the door that would lead into the backyard and opened it. The door opened wider—blown by the howling wind. She rushed out ahead of the trio and moved to the small shed in their backyard.

She pulled open the doors and withdrew two shovels from within. As she turned to Donatello and his goons, she realized they were already moving to the back of her backyard.

"Where are you going?" she asked, moving after them. She blinked away raindrops as the rain came down harder. The downpour quickly soaked her clothes and hair.

The two goons followed Donatello into the woods behind Miranda's house. She rushed to catch up, the sound of Jackson 5's

'One More Chance' playing in her head as she shielded her eyes from the rain.

They moved deeper into the woods until Donatello felt they were completely hidden from view. The goons dropped George's body with no remorse. George's body slammed into the mud with a thud.

Miranda gasped and the goon closest to her shrugged sheepishly.

Donatello took a shovel from Miranda and threw it at the bulkier of the two goons. The skinnier goon politely took the other shovel from her.

"Dig," Donatello told them.

Miranda moved to his side. "I wish you'd brought an umbrella."

He eyed her. "You're a killer now, sweetheart, just like me…We don't need umbrellas. At the end of the day, we're going to burn in Hell. We can use all the water we can get right now."

Miranda swallowed hard and crossed her arms over her chest, trying to preserve some warmth. She looked at George's body and realized that she'd murdered the father of her only child.

Around her, the thunderstorm raged on. The winds howled through the trees and the windchill made her shiver.

After an hour, the two goons had dug a pretty sizeable hole. Donatello turned to her. "We don't need you to stay out here." Miranda didn't move. Donatello realized her eyes were locked on the grave that had been dug. He placed both hands on her shoulders and shook her slightly.

Miranda sucked in a breath and looked at him. She tried not to recoil from his touch. "Listen to me closely, Miranda. Go back to your house. Call Prue. She's asleep but she'll answer. You need a witness."

"But why?" she asked, confused.

"You have to call the police."

She pulled away. "Have you lost your mind?!"

"George is dead now, Miranda. What do you think is going to happen when he doesn't show up to work after a few days? Or what do you think is going to happen when his court date gets here? People are going to be asking questions and wanting answers. You have to get ahead of this."

She nodded. He was right, of course. "What do I say?"

"Tell them you and your husband had another fight. He beat you, again, and then took off."

"What about the blood? There's so much blood!"

"Say he broke the table," he told her. "I saw that, too. Yeah, he fell into the table and cut himself before he ran off into the night. After the police leave, give it a day or so and then file a missing person's report. We want to make sure you've documented all of this."

"Thank you, Donatello. I really—"

"Don't thank me until you pay me my money."

She nodded. "I'll go to the bank first thing in the morning and withdraw the money."

*"I'll have one of the boys to pick it up." He nodded back towards the house. "Now, **go**."*

Miranda nodded and ran back towards the house. She picked up the phone and called Prudence—rousing her from her sleep just as Donatello had told her.

Prue quickly got dressed and rushed over to her friend's house.

Miranda moved back to her backyard and left the back door open. She looked up at the sky and blinked as rain fell onto her face.

No, the rain didn't wash away her numbness. It didn't give her peace, either.

She'd killed George.

Miranda brushed her rain-soaked hair off her face and fell to her knees in the grass. In the next moment she pitched forward and lay in the grass.

She groaned and began to cry. "What have I done?" she whispered into the grass.

Somehow, she managed to turn on her back.

Prudence managed to make it across the street in the thunderstorm and moved onto Miranda's porch. She closed the umbrella and prepared to knock on the front door, but it opened on its own.

Prue's heart began to race. What was she walking into?

"Miranda?" she called, opening the door wider. She cautiously moved into the dark house and held her umbrella up as a weapon.

Prue closed the front door and reached for the light switch. Light flooded the entrance way and she moved into the house.

Prue entered the living room and caught sight of the shattered table and all of the blood. She gasped.

"Miranda!?" she called, suddenly frantic. "Oh, God, what has George done to her now?"

Prue caught sight of the opened back door and rushed outside. She found Miranda lying in the grass—in the rain.

Without another thought, Prue ran outside and fell to her knees, pulling Miranda to a sitting position. "Miranda? Miranda, honey, are you okay?"

At first, Miranda didn't seem to recognize Prue and her brow creased in confusion. "Prue, is that you?"

"Yes, honey, I'm here. Are you hurt? Are you okay?" Prue observed the swelling on her friend's face and figured there were probably other bruises, too. "He beat you, again, didn't he?"

Miranda looked at her friend and nodded.

"Where's George now?"

"He's gone," Miranda replied, and it was the truth. He was gone and he wasn't coming back.

"Let's get you back in the house. We're calling the cops." Prue rose to her feet and helped Miranda back into the house.

"Miss?" called Detective Burns.

Miranda blinked. "I'm sorry?"

"I asked you a question," he told her. "You just sat there spaced out...It was almost like your mind was somewhere else for a moment."

She exhaled and looked at him. Her mind *had been* somewhere else. She'd recalled that fateful night when her life had changed...for the better.

It wasn't too difficult to dodge the detectives' questions once she'd learned the tricks.

Instead of answering them directly, she told them drawn-out accounts of the abuse she'd suffered at George's hands. She told them of the trips to the emergency room. She told them about her broken ribs and the broken arm. She told them about the black eyes and busted lips. She told them about the coma he'd put her in.

George was dead and there was no need for them to look for him.

Chapter 7

Prue walked through the doors of the Ritz-Carlton in New York fresh from her flight. She had a modeling gig tomorrow and had decided to get in town early so she'd have enough time for a massage.

Her Louis Vuitton purse hung on the elbow joint of her right arm. She wore a sleeveless, black Chanel dress and matching shades.

Strutting through the lobby as if she owned the place, Prue headed to the front desk—turning heads as she did so.

I might be HIV positive, but I've still got it, she thought to herself, *for now.*

She needed to call her doctor and see about her options when it came to medication.

Prue placed her bag on the counter and the front desk attendant eyed her. "Cameron comma Prudence," she said. "Checking in."

"Right away," said the front desk attendant. He grinned and flashed a dimple. The man took a step back from his screen. "Looks like you're already checked in, *Miss* Cameron."

Prue noted the emphasis on the miss. "It's *Missus* Cameron. I'm not divorced...yet." She brushed her long hair back. "But I can't be checked in, already. As you can see, I've only just arrived."

"Let me grab your keys. Any luggage?"

"One of the bell boys is bringing it up," she replied. The attendant nodded and moved down the counter for a moment to retrieve her room keys.

Prue pulled her shades off and wondered who'd checked her in already. Maybe her agent was finally doing his job and taking that extra step.

The attendant returned and handed her the keys. "You're in the Premiere Park View Suite."

Prue thanked him and then moved off to the elevator and rode it up to her room. She exited the elevator and headed down the hall until she was before the door that led into the redesigned corner suite with a panoramic view of Central Park and Sixth Avenue.

She opened the door and moved into the posh suite. She inhaled sharply as she marveled at the room's size and began to explore.

She placed her purse on an end table and then slid out of her black Christian Louboutin heels. A moment later, the bell hop arrived with her bags.

She gave him a $20 tip and closed the suite's door with her left hand. Suddenly, her wedding ring caught her eye.

Her marriage was in trouble. Everything had changed when Donatello had caught Romeo in their house.

She hadn't spoken to Donatello in days. He refused to return her calls and hadn't even come to Jack's funeral. She wondered where he was now.

Perhaps he was in New York for business, too. She reached for her purse and pulled her cellphone out.

"Hello, Prue."

She gasped—startled—and turned to find Romeo Lupe' in her suite. Her eyes grew wide and she placed a hand on her chest. "What the hell are you doing here? You nearly gave me a heart attack."

He held his hands out in an apparent apology. "I'm sorry. I didn't mean to startle you. I checked into the hotel for you, claiming to be your assistant. I figured we needed to talk, especially with how things ended between us."

"Why are you here?" she asked, moving towards him. "Who asked you to come to New York. Wait, *how* did you know I'd be here?"

"I called your agent and he told me."

"He's fired," Prue replied. She turned away from Romeo and began to text her agent.

Romeo grinned and took a seat. "I like your dress. It looks good on you."

"Gee, thanks. Just bought it," she sarcastically replied, rolling her eyes.

"So, what happened in Paris?" he asked her.

They needed to talk, but on her terms. He was way out of line here. But no time was better than the present.

She moved to the white couch in the sitting area and patted beside her. "Come have a seat."

He obeyed but didn't sit right next to her. He wore a simple gray shirt and distressed jeans, but still managed to look gorgeous in them. Romeo was a stunning man.

"Are you going to tell me what's going on, Prudence?" he asked, crossing his legs.

Prue was taken aback. He never called her by her full name. She cleared her throat. "Well, I went to the doctor and my report wasn't what I expected."

The corners of Romeo's mouth began to turn upward and then transformed into a dazzling smile. "You're pregnant?" He clapped his hands together. "Oh, please tell me we're having a baby?"

Prue's eyes grew wide and she waved her arms from side to side. "No, no, no, we're not having a baby! I'm not pregnant. I'm on the pill."

"Oh," he said, settling down. His expression quickly shifted. "So, what's wrong?"

"Romeo…there's no easy way to say this so I'll just say it." She placed her hands in her lap. "I tested positive for HIV."

A silence filled the suite and Romeo's face was frozen in shock. Prue searched his eyes for some kind of response, but one never came.

She waved her hand before his face. "Romeo? Please…tell me what you're thinking."

Romeo blinked and sucked in a breath. "*Wow*."

"I know right. Look, I'm going to get to the bottom of this. I just don't—"

"Prue," he said in a somber tone.

She stopped talking and looked at him. Suddenly, his eyes filled with an emotion that resembled regret.

Prue's eyes widened and realization filled her. She didn't have to get to the bottom of things anymore… She had her answer.

"*You? **You** gave me HIV?*"

"Prue, I'm sorry." He reached for her, but she pulled away. "I never intended to—"

"To WHAT, Romeo?! You gave me HIV! I *trusted* you! I trusted you with my body!"

"I know. It shouldn't have happened."

Tears began to fall despite her fury. "I cheated on my husband with you and all you can say is you're *sorry?*!" She shook her head and angrily wiped her tears away. "I'm young! This is a time for happiness and accomplishments, not divorces and planning for my own funeral!"

"Funeral?" he said. "Who said you're going to die? HIV is not a death sentence, at least not anymore. We aren't in the 80s, Prue. You're not going to die. You're going to live a long and healthy life, and I'll be right beside you. Donatello doesn't deserve you."

"And you think you do?!" She shook her head in anger. "So what, you decided to take it upon yourself to make sure no other man would ever want me?"

"That's not it either, Prue, and you know it! You know that I love you."

"Love me?!" Prue jumped to her feet. *"LOVE ME!?* Have you lost your mind? You don't destroy people you love! You don't *infect* people you love!" She screamed and knocked a pillow off the plush couch. She wished she had something harder to throw—like a chair. She wished she had something to swing—like a baseball bat.

"Prue, I know you hate me right now, but—"

"How long have you known?" she asked. Her voice had gone cold. She glared at him and Romeo averted his eyes. "Answer me," she said softly and when he didn't reply she yelled. "ANSWER ME!"

"Eighteen months," he answered.

Prue sucked in a breath through clenched teeth and felt her whole world shatter. Her heart sank and she felt her knees began to tremble.

Romeo had known longer than they'd been having an affair.

He'd *known!*

"How could you do this to me?" Fresh tears began to fall from her eyes. She didn't want to cry but couldn't help it. "How could you have unprotected *SEX* with me knowing that you were—"

"Why are you blaming me? You were there, too! You didn't ask for protection either?"

She slapped the couch. "So blame the victim, huh?! I'm to blame because you didn't wear a condom?! Take some responsibility in this!"

"You first," he muttered as he climbed to his feet and began to leave the hotel suite. But then he stopped and whirled around— jabbing a finger in her direction. "You played a part in this, too, Prue! You're not so innocent either."

"I'm not the one who infected someone else! You *knew* you were positive and you didn't even disclose that fact to me!" She began to pace the room but her knees continued to shake. She couldn't stand without bracing the wall. "It's illegal not to tell people you're positive, Romeo! It's a crime! This is how you repay me after all I've done for you? You hide the truth from me?! You risked my life!"

He scoffed. "*All you've done for me?*" He scoffed. "Who the hell do you think you are?"

"I'm the bitch who stayed by your side while you recovered!"

"It was your own fault I got shot in the first place!"

"You're unbelievable!" She shook her head and laughed—but it was humorless. There was no joy in it. There wasn't anything to be happy about. "How'd this happen?" She ran a hand through her hair and turned her eyes on Romeo.

He looked like the man she'd given up so much for, but he wasn't the same person—he couldn't be. The man she knew cared about her and wouldn't lie to her. The person before her wasn't a man—he was a coward.

"Do you mean who'd I get it from? Is that what you mean?" he asked.

She frowned. That hadn't crossed her mind, but now that he said it she wanted to know.

She'd meant how had he infected her? Was he not taking his medication? Had he ever taken medication?

She'd known people with HIV that were undetectable, but…

"Who gave you HIV, Romeo?" she asked, her voice low yet filled with pain.

She couldn't look at him. It hurt too much. She couldn't do anything.

A wave of nausea overcame her, and she leaned into the couch and pressed a hand to her forehead.

Romeo moved back towards the couch, his steps slow and deliberate. He waited until he took a seat on the couch opposite Prue.

"Kelsey Drake."

And the name slammed into Prue like a freight train. She felt like a dagger had sliced through her heart.

That name seemed to gut her and she felt her innards spill out onto the floor. Her world shattered.

Kelsey Drake?

The name echoed in her mind.

Kelsey Drake was gorgeous. Kelsey Drake was a former model turned photographer. Kelsey Drake was an icon in the fashion industry. Kelsey Drake worked for Vogue Italia as *the* top fashion photographer.

Kelsey Drake was a visionary. Kelsey Drake saw the world through a different lens.

Prue had worked with Kelsey Drake on a number of occasions. Kelsey Drake had booked Prue for two shoots last season.

Kelsey Drake was one of the first fashion photographers to call Prue a supermodel.

And Kelsey Drake had introduced her to Romeo.

But beyond that, Kelsey Drake was a *man.*

"You're kidding…right?" was all she could muster. Her chest suddenly felt tight. She couldn't breathe.

"I'm gay, Prudence…well, I suppose you could say I'm really bisexual."

There was a long pause.

Prue just stared at him in disbelief. She grew pale—blood draining from her face as her heart sunk. Her fingernails dug into the couch.

When Prue finally spoke, her voice was clear—devoid of emotion. "You're a heartless bastard, Romeo Lupe'."

"Prudence, you have to understand. I never wanted to hurt you. I care about you deeply. And clearly, I'm attracted to you…I mean, we couldn't have sex if I wasn't."

Prue felt bile rise and she covered her mouth. She couldn't throw up. She forced herself to look at him.

It had to be a joke, right? The universe had to be playing a cruel joke on her, right?

"Prue, I'm bisexual…Kelsey and I were together for six months, but it wasn't really a relationship... It was more like friends with benefits. What you and I have is something more... I'm sorry this had to happen. I'm sorry you had to find out this way."

"Sorry?" Her eyes began to bulge. "SORRY!?" she screamed. "Now you're sorry after you've slept with a man, infected me with HIV, and have gotten caught?! Why me, Romeo? What did I ever do to you?"

"You loved me."

She gasped. "Y-You…you *punished* me because I loved you?" She shook her head. "No, no, no. You don't love me. You love men. I mean, isn't that what you're telling me: that you love men and women? You slept with men? Wait, are you *still* sleeping with men?! Who else have you infected?"

"Prue, stop. Stop right there. I'm not some monster running around and sleeping with people and giving them this disease. You're the first person I've been with since Kelsey."

"Lucky me," she said sarcastically. She dabbed at her eyes. "No, you're a monster, Romeo."

"I'm not."

"I can't trust that. You lied, Romeo. You deceived me. You're a liar."

"I never lied. You never asked me if I was into guys. I just didn't tell the whole truth."

"A half-truth is still a lie, Romeo!" she shouted. "The lies! The LIES!" Tears streamed down her face. Sadness and anger collided within her and she began to vibrate from the strain the two emotions had on her.

She forced herself to her feet and moved to the window. She placed her forehead against the cool glass—she had a migraine now.

"How could I not know? How could I have been so stupid?" She turned from the window. "With all the gay people I've worked with in the industry, how could I not have known?! I fell for you! I broke my vows for you. How could I have been so stupid?"

Romeo moved towards her and tried to hug her and she fell into his arms. She'd lost herself for a moment, but when he reached up to wipe away her tears, she came to her senses. She shoved Romeo back and slapped him.

Romeo's eyes grew wide in shock and she slapped him again.

"Don't touch me! Don't you ever touch me again!"

"I swear I was going to tell you I had HIV."

"WHEN?!"

"When you left Donatello. I didn't want to put it all out there unless I was sure that you were going to leave him for me."

"Do you not hear yourself? Romeo, that's madness! I deserved to know! You gambled with my life and I lost!"

Her voice was trembling, and she had to get away from him. She moved towards the door, grabbed her purse, and ran out into the hallway.

She had to get out of there. She needed fresh air. She needed freedom.

Romeo had imprisoned her in darkness and she didn't want it to pull her under more than it already had. She had to get away.

"Prue!" came Romeo's voice as he rushed down the hall after her. "Prue, I can change!"

She reached the elevator and slammed a hand on the down button. She was forced to face Romeo as the elevator hadn't arrived by the time he reached her. "You can't take back what you've done."

"Prue, I love you. Please, don't leave me. Don't do this to us."

"ME?! I-I've done nothing! Romeo, don't you see what you've done?"

"All I've done is love you."

Prue blinked at the words. Did he really not get what he'd done? Did he not understand why she was upset?

"I love you, Prudence…Please, don't leave me."

Prue swallowed the bile that nearly came up again. She couldn't be here. Romeo was making her physically sick, but she had to face the truth.

"Honestly, I don't doubt that you love me…but the damage is done. I can never forgive you for what you've done. You lied to me, Romeo, and you've changed the course of my life against my will."

"So where does this leave us?"

A ding sounded, and the elevator doors opened. Prue stepped in but held up a hand. "Don't follow me." She averted her eyes and pressed the button for the lobby. "I don't know where this leaves us, Romeo, but I can't do this right now."

The doors began to close but Romeo reached out and caught the door. "Just say you love me. We can get you treatment, you'll leave Donatello, and things will be as they were."

She scoffed. "Things will *never* be as they were."

"You love me, Prue. I know you do. Please, let's just go back to your room and talk about this."

"No, I don't want to talk right now. I'm furious! You betrayed my trust."

"And you betrayed your husband."

Prue was taken aback. She took a step back and pressed the button for the lobby again.

"I'm sorry, Prue. I shouldn't have said that."

"Leave me alone."

Romeo sighed heavily and removed his hand from the doorway. The elevator doors slowly began to close. "Call me."

"I won't," she told him, and she meant it. "Now, I have to fight for my life because of a decision you made for me. You took away my choices in life, Romeo."

He stopped the elevator from closing again and it beeped loudly. "Prue, I—"

"People all around the world—*women* and *men*—are fighting for their lives against a disease that ravages their body all because of loving someone like *YOU!*"

"Who am I, Prue?" He released the elevator doors and they began to close again.

"You're a monster, Romeo. You're a sadistic monster."

Chapter 8

❧ ❧ ❧ ❧ ❧ ❧ ❧ ❧ ❧ ❧

Rain Fres gazed out of the floor-length window of her Park Avenue condominium. She and Derrick had been in New York only a few days but were already settling in quite nicely.

She moved through the massive living room dressed in a simple knee-length wrap dress. Her hair hung about her shoulders. She also wore light make-up. It was nearly noon and she was all dolled up with nowhere to go.

She looked like she belonged in the condo. She looked like she belonged in New York City, but did she really?

Derrick and Rain had arrived in the city a few days ago and Rain realized that the movers had already situated the furniture. However, it was none of the furniture she'd shipped up here.

No, everything was different. She hadn't picked it out—Derrick had. When she'd asked him about it Derrick had told her that he'd sold most of their old possessions—furniture included—in order to make room for more upscale décor.

Instead of going off, she said nothing. What could be done? If all had been sold and taken from her, what could she do?

She was here on her husband's dime.

Perhaps she'd made a grave error in coming here. Nothing was the same and everything had seemed to have changed overnight.

Derrick seemed to have changed from a laid back and down to earth individual to a pompous music producer who was entirely too full of himself. What had changed?

Had being in the city awakened something in her husband? He seemed so at ease here and less on edge than he had been in recent months.

Even now after having a few days to get used to it, being without most of her favorite possessions bothered her. She felt so uncomfortable in this new world that didn't seem to belong to her. This was Derrick's dream—not hers.

Perhaps Rachel had been right…

Nearly everything she'd picked out at their old Lyfe Road home had been replaced with newer, more expensive items.

Most surprisingly was the fact that her comfy sweat pants and oversized shirts—her 'relaxation' clothes—had "accidentally" been lost during the move. Derrick had replaced those items with exercise gear.

Was he trying to tell her something? Had she gained too much weight? Did he no longer love her curves?

Even now, what message was he trying to articulate by creating a home for them that didn't feel like a home?

Rain had no idea how she was going to find work here. The city was so huge and she had no connections here.

Did Derrick expect her to become a housewife?

Rain gazed out the large window and took in her surroundings. Hundreds of people populated the sidewalks. This was truly the city that never slept.

In her hands Rain held a coffee mug and raised it to her lips, taking in the warm liquid. Thoughts raced through her mind. She felt conflicted.

Who was she in this marriage?

She realized that Derrick had bought a condominium without even showing it to her. He hadn't asked for her blessing or approval. And come to think of it, when he'd been offered the position at Star BMG he hadn't consulted her on that, either.

Rain had simply showed up at their old house and had discovered that he was packing everything. It hadn't even crossed his mind that she was a part of this.

Derrick Fres still moved as though he were a single man with no one to be responsible to.

Rain frowned and took another sip from her mug. When had she relinquished her life to Derrick? When had she given Derrick permission to take charge of the direction of their lives?

Suddenly Rain realized that without even knowing it she'd turned into a woman she didn't recognize. She'd given up her life for Derrick and now, what did she have?

Perhaps Rachel was right. She'd told her this could happen…She'd warned Rain, but—

Rain shook her head and tried to push their conversation out of her mind but couldn't. She couldn't start second guessing herself and her marriage…could she?

Rain suddenly felt uneasy. Derrick now controlled both of their lives. How had she let that happen?

She'd been an independent woman for so long…how had she simply given her husband control of her life? It had all happened seamlessly.

Her name wasn't even on the condo. She had no rights here. If Derrick decided he was tired of her, she couldn't fight him. It was *his* condo.

Even when they'd gotten married, she'd signed a prenup. She hadn't been offended when Derrick had mentioned it in passing.

Rain had thought it a way to prove that she loved Derrick and only him. She didn't want his money. But now she began to even think about that decision.

Had she yielded to Derrick back then? Had that been when she'd relinquished control? Had that been the beginning?

Rain shook her head again because now that she wasn't working, all she had to rely on was her savings account. If that ran out before she could get a job, then what would she do?

Derrick was now the sole bread winner in their house. Would she have to ask him for money? Would he give her an allowance? A stipend?

Was she now solely reliant on her husband?

An uneasiness washed over Rain. Suddenly she didn't feel safe anymore. This wasn't what she'd bargained for at all.

She wasn't this person. She didn't recognize the person she'd become.

Rain had once been independent and now she saw where Derrick had made her *dependent.*

Heat rushed her cheeks and she blushed in embarrassment.

How pathetic, she thought to herself.

Something just didn't feel right. *This* didn't feel right.

Suddenly, arms wrapped around her waist and she jumped. She hadn't even heard Derrick approach her.

"Are you okay?" he asked, speaking close to her left ear.

"I was just thinking, that's all," she told her husband as he pulled her closer to his body. Rain instinctively wrapped her arms around his and inhaled. The scent of his cologne filled her nostrils.

He was wearing the cologne she liked the least.

"You look so beautiful," he told her. Rain felt his cheeks move as he smiled against her neck. She started to twist in his arms to face him, but he turned her back towards the window. "I just want to look at you."

"Derrick—"

But that was all she was able to manage before she felt a hardness against her backside. "You smell so good," he said, his voice deep as he whispered in her ear.

A shiver ran down Rain's spine. He sounded so gruff—so unlike himself.

He kissed the back of her neck and pressed her against the glass of the floor-to-ceiling window. Rain had been unsure at first but now she knew that he was hard.

"Derrick," she said, trying to laugh off the anxiety that was building in her chest. "Let's go upstairs." She tried to move but couldn't—he kept his arms wrapped around her body.

"Stay right here," he told her. His voice was strong and clear. "I want you right now."

Usually Derrick was a tender lover, but right now, he was another person. It was as if just being in New York had brought about a change in him.

Rain tried to move her hands, but he reached out and grabbed one of them. She dropped the coffee mug and it shattered on the hard wood floor.

"Don't worry about it. We'll get a maid to clean it up." Derrick kissed her neck again.

"We don't have a—"

"We will." He grabbed her hand and placed it over her head.

Rain went still all over. "Derrick, I don't want to—"

"Just relax." With his free hand, he pulled up her dress.

"No, Derrick," she whispered, panicking. It was broad daylight. Surely people could see them through the window.

But beyond that, she didn't want to have sex. She didn't want this, and he wouldn't let up. She tried to pull away but he squeezed her wrists—pinning her in place against the floor-to-ceiling window.

Rain struggled against Derrick, but that only made his grip tighten on her hands. He quickly reached down and unzipped his pants and then lifted her dress up again.

When he entered her from behind, she gasped and tried to push off the window, but couldn't. "Derrick!" she cried out. "Derrick, wait! I—"

It had been so long since they'd last had sex and she wasn't ready for him. A sharp pain ripped through her and he shoved the rest of his manhood inside of her.

Exhaling in ecstasy, Derrick began to slam into her. Rain cried out and was pressed against the window. Her cheek rubbed into the glass.

"Derrick, stop," she told him, but he ignored her. He thrust against her as she stared out into the street. Rain felt a dampness on her cheek and realized that she was crying.

Her husband took her body and slammed into her relentlessly. Rain simply couldn't believe what was happening.

She tried to focus on anything but the moment. She glanced down at the people on the sidewalk heading to their many destinations. She caught sight of a mother and her toddler. They were probably headed to a midday Mommy and Me class.

Rain turned her head and caught sight of a condo across the street. A young man danced around his living room in his boxers. He smiled and swayed to the rhythm of a song Rain couldn't hear.

She tried to focus on anything other than the pain...other than the betrayal of her devotion.

How much time had passed?

Was he almost done?

Derrick had never forced himself on her before...but there was a first time for everything.

The city had brought about a change in him.

Or perhaps he'd always been this way and I simply hadn't noticed, Rain thought to herself.

Derrick groaned in her ear and Rain knew he was close to climaxing. She sobbed and watched as a tear rolled down the glass— her face was smushed that much into the glass. He came with a loud groan that seemed to echo throughout their condominium.

Rain stifled a whimper as Derrick relaxed against her body, pressing her further into the glass window. He panted and then pulled out of her.

Rain gasped as a new stab of pain shot through her pelvis at the quickness with which he withdrew from her.

In the next moment, Derrick turned her around and kissed her.

His eyes were closed, and Rain felt as though she was looking at a stranger. He pressed his lips against hers, but she didn't yield her mouth to him.

Derrick opened his eyes and then realized she was crying. "What's wrong with you?" he asked as he began to frown.

She pushed him aside and rushed up the rail-less stairs and into the master bedroom.

Rain locked herself in the bedroom and rushed to the bathroom, pulling her clothes off as sobs broke out of her. She turned on the shower and quickly climbed in.

The sound of the shower drowned out her sobs as she began to scrub her skin. She'd never felt so filthy in her life.

As the suds circled the drain, Rain wondered if she should leave. She didn't know the man that had just taken her body.

But where would she go? Should she return to Lyfe Road? Maybe she could stay with Rachel.

But then what would her friends think? She couldn't tell them that her husband had raped her, could she? He wasn't a stranger. He didn't hold a gun to her head. He hadn't abducted her...He was her husband!

But it was rape nonetheless.

Derrick had gotten off and she'd gotten violated.

Rain sank to her knees in the shower and cried. She covered her mouth to muffle the sound.

What had gotten into Derrick? And what was happening to her?

Eventually, the water turned cold and Rain forced her body out of the shower. She moved into the master bedroom and caught sight of the door.

Adrenaline flooded her as fear gripped her heart. She knew she'd locked the door. Had Derrick kicked it open?

She rushed to the door, closed it, and locked it again. Then, she rushed to her cellphone—it was still on the nightstand next to her side of the bed.

Should I call the police? She wondered and then changed her mind. She was too embarrassed. Husbands didn't rape their wives.

The cops would just say she was trying to get back at him by filing a report.

Rain started to place her phone back down, but then the screen glowed. Rain pulled the phone to her face and realized she had two missed calls from her cousin.

Rain's cousin, Patricia "Patty" Warren, was twenty-four and the daughter of her Aunt Karen—the woman who'd raised Rain after her parents' tragic car accident. Rain had then moved in with her aunt and two cousins—Patty & Anne—in a small two bedroom duplex in Liverpool. Though it had been extremely tough on Karen as a single mother raising her own kids and now her niece, she did the best she could until she fell into a coma several years ago.

Rain hadn't seen Patty or Anne since her last visit to the UK. But after what had happened between her and Derrick, she needed to get away. Perhaps this had been a sign from God.

Did she need to run? Should she talk to Derrick about what had happened? Did she need closure or did she just need to leave?

What was the protocol for being raped?

Rain tapped the screen and called her cousin back. A few moments later, a soft British accent filled Rain's ear.

"Hey, Patty, I just saw your missed call."

"Rain Dewitt!" exclaimed Patty, her accented voice filling Rain's ear.

Rain was forced to smile at the reminder of the maiden name she'd left behind—the name that belonged to her father; the name that her mother had taken when she'd removed 'Warren' from her surname.

"It's Rain Fres now," she said and then wondered if life was telling her that it needed to return to Dewitt. Was the universe trying to tell her something?

Derrick wasn't a bad man; at least she didn't think he was. But something had changed within him.

Something had broken inside of him. Something had turned him into a monster.

"Hello?" called a voice and Rain remembered that she'd been on the phone.

She shook her head. "I'm sorry. I spaced out for a moment."

"It's alright. How've you been?"

"I should be asking you the same thing, Patty! We haven't talked in ages."

"I've been great. Lonely, but great. Ever since Anne left home and moved to Paris I've been alone in the duplex."

"You're still staying there?"

"It's always been home, Rain, and it always will be. I wouldn't dare sale it. What if mom wakes up?"

Rain was silent for a moment. That was a good question. If her Aunt Karen woke up tomorrow, she'd expect to return to the duplex. That's all she'd ever known.

"You're right," Rain replied. "But I was returning your call. You called twice. Is everything okay?"

"Yeah, I was cleaning out the attic the other day—I was bored, don't judge me—and found something. I came across a small trunk, and you know me, I'm always so curious."

"What was in the trunk, Patty?" Rain asked, uninterested in her cousin's discovery.

"I found *letters*, Rain."

Rain frowned to herself and wrapped the towel tighter around her body. "Were they addressed to me or...? I mean, I don't understand why you were calling, Patty."

"Yes, the letters are addressed to you," Patty replied, but she sounded sad all of a sudden.

"Patty, what is it? What's wrong? Who are the letters from?"

Rain heard her cousin inhale and then Patty spoke. "Rain, the letters are from your father."

Rain froze. *My father?* She thought.

She swallowed hard. Yes, clearly the universe was trying to tell her something. Even her father was reaching out to her from the afterlife. She even heard Whoopi Goldberg's character from *Ghost* speaking in her head: ***Rain, you're in danger, girl!***

"Rain, did you hear me?"

"Yes, Patty," she replied, her voice clear.

"Do you want them? I can mail them to you."

Rain looked over her shoulder and made sure that the door was still locked. "No, don't mail them... I'll come and get them."

Rain now knew that this was a sign for her to get out.

Chapter 9

જ્જ્જ્જ્જ્જ્જ્જ્જ્જ્

Rain left the condo that same day. She took an overnight bag and only packed the essentials—her passport among them. She left everything else behind, her wedding ring included.

Rain had watched Miranda suffer at the hands of her abusive husband and knew that she would never stand for it. It had only taken one time for Derrick to flip the script and she was gone.

She was still in disbelief that he'd pressed her against the window and raped her. Who was that man? That wasn't the same man she'd married nearly two years ago. That wasn't the man she thought she'd come to love.

Twelve hours later, Rain's plane touched down in Liverpool and she hailed a cab to the small duplex. While she sat in the backseat of the cab, she took a moment to send a text to each of her best friends. She notified Prue, Rachel, Miranda, and Freya that she had left Derrick and was in the UK.

She regretted revealing so much as soon as she hit send. Moments later, her phone buzzed as Freya called her. Rain let it ring. She wasn't ready to talk about it.

She couldn't.

She needed more time to process everything that was going on. The phone continued to vibrate in her hand.

When the call went away she sent a second text letting them know she was safe and wasn't ready to talk about it, yet. She told them she'd contact them when she was ready to talk. Miranda sent her a reply saying "I'm praying for you. Xoxo."

Rain grinned at the text and placed her phone back in her purse.

She looked at her watch. Derrick was probably on his way home from the studio. She wondered what he'd think when he found her wedding ring lying on the kitchen counter.

Would he think she'd left him, or would he think she'd just accidentally left it behind after washing her hands?

It didn't matter to Rain. Either way, she was out.

The cab arrived at the duplex and Rain headed up the cracked driveway. It still looked the same.

She rang the doorbell and glanced at the small lawn where she and Anne had played with their dolls as children. She looked at the sidewalk and remembered falling off her bike when her aunt had first taught her how to ride it.

This place was filled with so many memories.

The door creaked open and Rain turned to find her cousin standing there. Patty grinned and squealed with excitement.

Rain couldn't help but smile. Patty was 5'6" and wore a simple t-shirt and jeans. Her hair was pulled back in a ponytail.

"Rain, you're here!" cried Patty.

The two women embraced in a tight hug, but Rain didn't let it last to long. The second her cousin wrapped her arms around her, she was reminded of Derrick touching her and pushing her into the window.

Rain awkwardly pulled away and her cousin stepped aside to let her into the house. All she wanted to do was be shown to the trunk and read the letters from her father.

What were they about? Why had he written them?

"How was your flight?" Patty asked as she led Rain into the small living room.

Rain was surprised that it still looked much the same as it had in her childhood.

"The flight was fine. I mostly slept." She recalled the Xanax she'd taken and how relaxed she'd been.

"It's so good to have you here." Patty plopped on the couch. Rain placed her bags on the floor and took a seat beside her. "I've readied the room for you. Would you like something to eat or do you need rest?"

"I'd like to see the letters," Rain said, honestly. And then she realized that might've come out rude. She looked at her cousin. "Please," she added with a grin.

Patty patted her cousin's lap and headed out of the room. She returned moments later with a small trunk that resembled a treasure chest.

Rain realized she'd been holding her breath and exhaled. Patty placed the trunk on the couch between them and then turned to her cousin. She cocked her head. "Are you alright?"

Rain tore her eyes from the brown trunk. "Why do you ask?"

Patty shrugged. "You just look so sad."

Rain smiled sadly. "This is a lot," she told her. And in truth, finding out about these letters was a lot, but she also had dozens of other emotions coursing through her. She was traumatized by Derrick's actions and couldn't even put into words what she was feeling.

"Do you want to open it?" Patty asked, gesturing at the trunk. Rain nodded and when she didn't reach to open the trunk, Patty opened it for her.

Rain sucked in a breath. There were about a dozen letters in the trunk and a few pictures. She reached for the framed pictures and realized they were pictures of her with her parents. One was from her third birthday. Another was from her first day of kindergarten.

Rain felt the floodgates open and tears began to fall. Her heart ached for her parents. She mourned them and Patty reached out for her.

Rain held up a hand. "I'm okay. I'm okay." She really didn't want to be touched.

Patty pulled back and held her hands up in mock surrender. "How about I just give you a moment alone, yeah?" She rose from the couch and exited the living room.

Patty busied herself in the kitchen as Rain went through the trunk. Finally, Rain pulled the stack of letters from the trunk and glanced at the first one. The first letter was postmarked for June 11, 1993.

Rain closed her eyes and exhaled. That was only a few weeks before her parents had died in the car accident. The letter was addressed to her in her father's handwriting. She rubbed her thumb over the letters.

Rain rose off the couch and began to pace the living room. She was too nervous to open the letter. She hadn't seen her father's handwriting in years.

Why was so much happening in such a short time?

She thought about Derrick and her life back home in the States. She wasn't happy anymore…especially not after what had happened. She knew she wasn't going to return to New York. She never wanted to see Derrick again.

Perhaps these letters represented a sign? Maybe it was time for her to return to the UK?

Rain heard footsteps behind her and turned to find Patty heading back into the room with two cups in her hand. "I brought tea."

Rain grinned and reached for a cup. She instantly felt the warmth from the mug. But just as quickly as her grin had appeared on her face, it disappeared as flashes of the coffee mug she'd held in her hand when Derrick had raped her filled her mind.

Rain cleared her throat and placed the cup on the mahogany coffee table before her.

Patty eyed her wearily and took a seat on the couch. "I don't mean to pry, but are you sure you're okay? Even before I got the trunk, you just seemed heavy. Are you sure everything is alright?"

Rain took a seat. She didn't answer her immediately. "There's a lot going on in my life right now."

"We can talk about it." Patty reached out to touch Rain's shoulder. Rain flinched but didn't pull away. She forced her eyes to focus on her cousin. "You can talk to me, Rain."

Rain shook her head and Patty withdrew her touch. "It's just the letters, that's all. I promise. It's brought up a lot of old emotions." She wasn't ready to share what had happened to her.

"How about we open one?" Patty asked and she reached for one before Rain could answer her.

"No," Rain said, her voice clear. "Not yet." Patty froze and placed the letter down.

Rain didn't feel right holding the truth back from her cousin. Patty was her family. She reached for her cousin's hand and Patty looked at her. Worry crossed Patty's face in the next moment and Rain's eyes watered. "Everything isn't alright…"

"What's going on?"

"All of this has been a godsend. I wanted to get away and then you called me about the letters. It was the perfect opportunity."

Patty cocked her head. "What are you running from?"

"Not *what,* Patty, but *who*?"

"Alright…" Patty cleared her throat. "W*ho* are you running from?"

"My husband."

Chapter 10

Rachel Richards walked through the silent halls of her empty home. She stared at her cellphone. She'd text Rain twice to check on her and she hadn't yet responded. Perhaps she was resting.

How many hours was Liverpool ahead of them? Rachel couldn't calculate the time difference.

She ran a hand along the corners of the picture frames that lined the wall leading down the stairwell. She stopped at one of Jack's pictures and smiled. "I miss you, Jack."

Suddenly, the doorbell rang and Rachel glanced in the direction of the front door. She wasn't expecting company.

She looked herself over and frowned. She was dressed in pajamas and wore her soft pink robe.

Rachel shrugged and closed her robe as she descended the stairs. She was still in mourning. She was allowed to look a mess.

Rachel unlocked the door and then pulled it open and was amazed to find a familiar face there.

The lady from the funeral, Rachel thought to herself.

The woman stood there, her hair blowing in the breeze. She wore a purple dress with black pumps. Her eyes were piercing and her lips were thin but colored red.

"Can I help you?" Rachel asked, taking the woman in. She suddenly felt self-conscious in her pajamas.

"Hi, I know you don't know me, but I was at—"

"Jack's funeral," Rachel said, cutting the woman off.

"Yes," the woman replied, grinning. She was probably in her late 20s or early 30s. Rachel wasn't sure. She quickly took the woman in and judged her. She was in need of a fresh dye job—her roots were coming in with a dull brown. She was a little wide in the hips and—

"I remember you," Rachel said as she pulled herself from her thoughts. She tried to keep her voice light but found herself immediately on the defensive. She crossed her arms over her chest.

How'd this woman find her? How did she know where Rachel lived?

"What can I do for you?" Rachel asked again, trying to figure out what the woman wanted.

"My name is Robin Martez... I need to talk to you."

Rachel rose an eyebrow. "About?" She knew the answer before the woman even opened her mouth to respond.

"Jack."

Rachel closed her eyes and she felt her irritation growing. *What did you do, Jack?*

"Do you mind if I come in?" Robin Martez asked. "I promise I won't take up too much of your time."

Rachel placed a hand on her forehead. Anxiety began to grip her chest. "I-I need to have a seat." Rachel left and moved into her living room—leaving the door wide open.

Robin's face twisted in confusion. She looked around to see if anybody in the neighborhood was paying attention then she walked into the house and closed the door behind her.

Robin looked around, surprised at how elegant the house looked. "Hello?" she called, her heels sounding on the wooden floorboards.

"In here," replied a voice filled with grief. Robin followed the sound of the voice and found Rachel in the kitchen sitting at the granite countertop. Rachel poured herself a glass of Pinot noir.

"Um, Mrs. Richards—"

"Well, come on in and take a seat. Would you like a glass?"

Robin shook her head 'no'. "It's barely ten o'clock."

Rachel chuckled dryly. "Is it?" She pushed a bar stool out from the countertop. "Have a seat."

"Mrs. Richards—"

"Call me *Rachel*," Rachel said, her eyes vacant as she spoke in a voice barely above a whisper. "That *other* name is too painful."

Robin simply stood there, gazing at a woman whose eyes were unfocused, as if staring at something in the distance. Robin moved towards the countertop and took a seat next to Rachel.

"Please...*Rachel,* we should talk."

Rachel snapped out of it at that moment and looked at the woman. "You want to talk about Jack?" Robin nodded and Rachel continued. "How did you know him? I mean, I know he was a football star, but did you actually know him? And how did you find me?"

"I used to be a cheerleader in the league."

Rachel stared at her intently. She reached for her wine glass and took another sip. Robin simply sat there, staring back.

"Is that it? You two were co-workers and you've come to offer your condolences?" Rachel rose to her feet. "You could've offered your condolences at the funeral. I'll show you out now."

Rachel turned to leave the living room and Robin rose to her feet. "I slept with Jack."

Rachel froze in place and closed her eyes. She was thankful that her back was to the woman. She didn't want her to see that she was struggling not to cry.

Even in death Jack betrayed her. He'd had plenty of indiscretions, but they'd had a silent agreement that he was never to bring them to their house. Those sluts were never to know where he lived. How had this one slipped through the cracks?

Rachel put on a brave face and turned to the woman. "You show up on my doorstep—unannounced I might add—and decide to come clean about sleeping with a married man? Why? Why share that information with Jack's widow? Did you think I needed more pain in my life?"

Robin shook her head. "I never meant to—"

"What did you come here for then?" Rachel asked sternly, her patience stretched thin.

"I was young. I didn't know the severity of my actions. I mean, I was really, *really* young and stupid and—"

"Seems like you still are."

Robin was taken aback. "I'm not a bad person. You have to believe me."

"I believe that you were young and pretty, and I'll admit that you still are, but you haven't learned from your mistakes. You shouldn't have come here. Please leave, now."

"I loved him."

Rachel's eyes grew wide. That was *it!* This bimbo thought that she'd been in love with Jack. Rachel rushed across the kitchen and slapped Robin as hard as she could.

Robin yelped and her face twisted with the blow.

"GET **OUT!**" Rachel shouted, her voice dripping with venom.

Robin straightened up and glared at Rachel. She exhaled out of her nose sharply and clenched her jaw. "That hurt."

"Good," Rachel replied curtly. She pointed towards the front door. "Now GET THE FUCK OUT OF MY HOUSE!"

Robin didn't move. "Mrs. Richards, I know you may hate me, but we still need to talk. You need to know what happened between your husband and I."

Rachel slapped her again. "Get out of my house, you disrespectful slut!"

Robin threw her hair back and touched her jaw. "Jack fathered my child."

Rachel felt like she'd been struck by a train. She took a step back and suddenly recalled the child that had been at the woman's side at the funeral.

"Jack and I carried on with our affair for nearly three years until I left the Packers cheerleading squad in late 2003."

Rachel moved past Robin and grabbed the wine glass. She chugged the rest of the wine and then poured herself another glass.

"Drinking isn't going to change the fact that I had your husband's baby."

Rachel took a seat at the countertop again and Robin moved towards her.

"I told Jack I was pregnant. He insisted that I have an abortion and I wouldn't…So I quit the squad and he set me up in a condominium." Rachel closed her eyes and sighed. That sounded so much like Jack. He was so quick to fold when under pressure. "He would send me money every month. He made sure we were taken care of."

Suddenly, Rachel realized where this was going. Robin hadn't come to gloat. She looked up and frowned. "So, now that he's gone you think I'm going to continue to foot the bill?" She laughed but the sound wasn't filled with joy. "How can you live with yourself? How can you live with the fact that you *slept* with my husband and gave birth to his bastard?!"

Robin crossed her arms over her chest. "Don't you dare call my child a bastard."

"Fuck your child!" shouted Rachel. "How *dare* you show your face at this house?!" Her eyes grew wide. "At his *funeral?!* Do you know no shame?"

"I had every right to be there!"

"Get the hell out of my house!" Rachel shouted and she threw her half-full glass of wine at Robin. Robin jumped back and the glass shattered at her feet.

Robin glared at her. "You're just upset that I gave Jack the one thing you never could!"

Rachel froze. Robin had struck a chord. Had Jack revealed their fertility issues to his mistress?

None of that mattered now. He was dead.

Rachel forced herself off the stool and moved across the kitchen. Robin instantly turned and headed towards the front door. "You're not going to get a dime from me!" Rachel shouted as she chased Robin out of the house.

She slammed the front door and began to shake—nearly hysterical as tears fell. She screamed and thrashed about, knocking over an end table before she rushed through the living room. She knocked over a picture, threw a pillow, and then turned her sights on the stairwell. She grabbed every picture of Jack and hurled them to the ground. Glass shattered and she fell to her knees on the stairwell.

Rachel was red in the face and screamed until her throat was sore.

Jack Richards, the love of her life, had not only died on her, but had left her alone.

Still, after all the years they'd been married, Jack still hid secrets from her. But to fund his mistress's life and take care of their secret child was beyond her.

Rachel wiped her eyes and wondered if Robin had still been sleeping with Jack when he had contracted Hepatitis C.

Maybe she'd die, too.

Chapter 11

Freya Goodchild, the estranged wife of Aaron Goodchild, walked through the glass doors of Goodchild Law Firm. She was on her lunch break from her new job at a local advertising firm. Though she'd kicked him out of the family home, told him she was pregnant, and had told him she'd wanted a divorce, she hadn't yet told him she was pregnant with twins.

He needed to know. He also needed to be served with divorce papers—she'd filed just the other day.

Freya wore a green dress with nude heels. Her hair hung about her shoulders in waterfall curls.

Today was the beginning of the end. The children weren't adjusting too well to their father being out of the house, and Freya didn't understand that. Yes, for most of their lives he'd been in the home, but he hadn't actually been *present*. Freya shook her head and tightened the hold on the envelope in her hand.

Freya headed to the reception desk and leaned against it. "Good morning, Cynthia," Freya said, grinning at the young blonde at the desk. "I'm here to see Mr. Goodchild."

Cynthia smiled and informed Freya that her husband was in a meeting, but she was welcome to wait in his office. Freya thanked her and then moved past the reception desk and headed down the carpeted corridor.

Cynthia suddenly looked up and searched for Freya. "Mrs. Goodchild, I—" But Freya was out of earshot. The receptionist reached for the phone and quickly dialed Aaron's secretary. "Inform Mr. Goodchild that his wife is on her way up…Yes, yes, I know, but I didn't have time to stop her!"

On the fifth floor, the elevator dinged open and Freya stepped off. She passed portraits of the partners—past and present—and then finally came to a portrait of her late father-in-law. Aaron's father had died of a heart attack nearly a year ago. Next to his portrait was Aaron's.

A few feet past the portrait was the first set of double doors that led into Aaron's suite. Freya pushed the first set of doors open and caught sight of Aaron's secretary, Ramona. Ramona was an older woman and that suited Freya just fine.

Ramona rose from her desk and made a beeline for Freya. "Mrs. Goodchild, can I—"

"I'm just here to see my husband." Freya moved around Ramona and headed towards the second set of doors. "It's good to see you, Ramona. How are the grandkids?"

"They're doing fine, but—"

Freya turned the knob of the second set of doors and opened the door. Freya's eyes widened as she caught sight of the back of her husband.

His pants were around his knees and sweat slickened his bare back. Freya watched in horror as he nailed a woman on the edge of his desk, her red-bottomed Christian Louboutin heels in the air.

"Aaron!" yelled Freya, more upset than saddened by his infidelity.

Aaron looked over his shoulder and his eyes grew wide with horror. "Freya!" He pulled out of the fair skinned woman and spun to face her—revealing that he'd entered this woman without protection. The woman sat up and Freya instantly recognized her.

"Hello, Greer," Freya said, her voice dry.

Greer Harris was a junior partner at the firm. She was young and Italian, hair cut short in a bob. She instantly began to pull her clothes on as Aaron pulled up his pants, grabbed his shirt, and moved towards his wife.

"Freya, it isn't what you think!" exclaimed Aaron as he stumbled across the room and buttoned up his shirt.

"So, you're saying I didn't just catch you nailing one of your co-workers on the desk that once belonged to your father?" Her voice was devoid of emotion.

Greer suddenly tried to flee the room, but Freya blocked her way. The woman wouldn't look her in the eye. "You know he has kids at home, don't you?" she asked.

"Freya, I'm sorry," Greer said, her head hung low. She then moved around Freya and rushed out of the office.

Aaron eyed his secretary. Ramona stood in the doorway, her eyes wide and her jaw open. "Don't you have work to do?!" he yelled. Ramona jumped and rushed back to her desk.

Freya moved further into the office and Aaron slammed the door shut. "Are you trying to knock her up, too?" Freya asked.

"Jesus, no! She's on the pill."

Freya laughed and spun to face the man who'd broken her heart. "I can't even be mad at you, Aaron. You're a dog."

"Now, wait a minute—"

She raised the envelope. "I just came to drop these off." She shoved the envelope in his chest and moved past him and towards the door.

"What is this?" he asked, opening the envelope.

She spun to face him, her hair whirling as she did so. "I filed for divorce the other day. Sign those, please. As a matter of fact, do it today."

"Freya, you can't be serious!"

She pulled off her wedding band and engagement ring and threw them both at him. He ducked and then looked at her, shocked. "I've never been more serious in my life!" She composed herself and exhaled. "I hate you, Aaron."

He was surprised at how even her voice was. She didn't sound angry. She only sounded like she'd just come to terms with the truth.

"You're allowed to fuck whoever you want. You're allowed to do whatever you want. You just won't be doing it to me anymore." She turned and left the room.

Aaron followed her out of the suite and his secretary pretended to busy herself with something else. "Freya! Freya, wait!"

Freya stopped and realized that other partners had come out of their offices to see what all the commotion was about.

Freya suddenly felt embarrassed. Aaron had shamed her in public. Ramona had seen the madness unfold, too. This affair and subsequent confrontation would be the talk of the office before the end of day.

"Let me talk to you for a minute," Aaron said, his face red as frustration filled him. He eyed his co-workers. "This doesn't concern you! Get back to work!" he shouted, and they began to move about the office, busying themselves with tasks.

Freya headed back into his office. Aaron straightened his tie and followed her, slamming the oak door behind him.

"Do you know what you've done?!" he shouted.

"Me?!" She scoffed and placed a hand on her hip. "You've got some nerve, Aaron! You're the one that was fucking some slut in your office!"

"And you're the one causing a scene at my job! If you had one, you'd know—"

"I do have one now," she replied curtly, crossing her arms over her chest.

"Well, I-I." Aaron always stuttered when he was at a loss for words.

Freya grinned but there was no joy in the action. "See, you thought I'd rely on you forever. You were *wrong*, Mr. Goodchild. Now look, I came here to serve you the divorce papers. Let's just sign them and—"

"You think it's going to be that easy? Freya, we have kids! I love you!"

She chuckled. "You can stop lying now, Aaron. It's over. Yes, we have kids, and yes, you'll be paying child support. You don't love me. We'll figure out the logistics during the court proceedings, but we both know you don't give a shit about our kids!"

"That's not true!" he replied, pacing the office. "Jesus, Freya! Everything is just so messed up now!"

"Guess who did that though? *You* did! You ruined us, Aaron, and now you're embarrassing us, too!" She exhaled. "What happened to you? What happened to *us*?"

He simply looked at her. "Nothing, Freya. We just grew apart."

"That's bull and you know it! What did I do to you to deserve for you to be an absentee parent and partner?!"

"I'm not! I've been—"

"You just started back doing what's right! You walk around like you're the king when you don't even treat your queen right! You lied to me once and we got pregnant! You lied, *again*, and now we're having twins!"

He shook his head. "What?" he asked, his voice low.

Freya looked away; she couldn't look at him. "I'm pregnant with twins."

He exhaled sharply. "That can't be true, can it? I-I mean…that's crazy. I can't believe we'll have seven kids."

"And now you're having an affair. Not to mention the fact that you're having unprotected sex with her! How long has this been going on? Do I need to get tested?"

"No! Why would you think—"

"The world has changed, Aaron! There are all kinds of diseases out there! Do you realize that you could've brought something home?"

He shook his head and ran a hand over his dirty blonde hair. "I wasn't thinking, Freya. It just kind of happened."

Freya stood there with her face etched in disbelief. "You've lost your mind, Aaron! How long has this been going on?"

"Six months," he replied, his voice low.

She scoffed again and slammed her palm on the chair in front of her. "*Six* months? If you really wanted to mess around, that was all you would've had to say! I promise I would've let you go. We could've gotten a divorce months ago, well really we could've gotten a divorce back at four kids!"

"This isn't all on me. I've changed, Freya…but so did you."

"Me? What did I do?"

"You started devoting more and more time to the kids and less to me."

"You realize that *you* gave me those children, right? I didn't lay there and make them all by myself."

"Let's not play the blame game," he told her.

"No, Aaron, *let's!* It doesn't work that way. See, you can dish it but you can't take it. You expect me to listen when all I'm hearing is you making excuses! What, do you expect me to stay when all you can say is 'I wasn't there for you?' Aaron, you're a grown ass man! I'm not your mother!"

"I never expected you to be my mother! Now, lower your voice!"

"I'm not yelling, I'm just telling you the truth! You're a sorry excuse for a man." She dropped her purse in a chair and crossed her arms.

"And you're just another angry black woman." He shook his head. "You must've bumped your head, coming in here and causing a scene like you're on Maury or something!"

Freya was taken aback. She opened her mouth, but nothing came to her. *Finally,* the ugly monster had reared its head.

"I wondered how long it would be before you started bringing race into it…You've probably always felt that way."

He looked at her and raised an eyebrow and he suddenly realized his mistake. He crossed the room and tried to touch her, but she took a step back.

"Nope, don't touch me." She cocked her head. "What, you think I'm just your whore, right? Or better yet do you think I'm your filthy white man's whore? Is that what you think of me, Aaron? You think I'm an angry black woman?"

"That's not what I think, Freya."

She smirked. "Oh, but you *said* it, Aaron. What other things do you think about the mother of your kids?" She held her hands up. "Better yet, save it for court. This conversation is really starting to bore me." She grabbed her purse and turned to leave.

"Freya, wait."

She stopped to face the stranger she'd been married to for nearly eleven years. "Yes, Aaron?"

He moved to the minibar in his office and poured himself a drink. He grabbed the glass and swirled the brown liquor in his hand before he took a sip. Freya assumed it burned on the way down by the face he'd made.

Finally, he looked at her. "You can have the kids. I'll agree to full custody."

"That only seems appropriate seeing as you don't know the first thing about parenting."

He grinned, but Freya realized that something had changed. He suddenly seemed colder. She took a step back—closer to the door. "I'll agree to child support, at a reduced amount…but that's *it*. I won't pay for the car or the house. You're on your own there."

Her heart sank. She knew he was a cold bastard, but she had not expected this. She simply smiled because she'd been prepared for the monster she knew was inside her husband—he was a lawyer after all. "That's fine, Aaron. I'm not some poor black woman on government assistance."

"But your mother is, right?" Aaron looked at her and grinned and then took a seat in one of the high back chairs in his office.

Freya's jaw dropped. He was going for the jugular. "Don't you *dare* talk about my mother like that! I'm not some hood rat you just found on the side of the road."

He laughed, and she could hear the evilness behind the sound. Aaron was going to give her hell in this divorce.

"I don't need anything from you, Aaron."

"Good," he replied. "Because you can scratch spousal support off your list, too. I'm not funding your life, Freya."

"Just take care of your children."

He waved her words off. "Oh, I will, just like I have for our entire marriage."

"I only came here today to give you the documents and to tell you something, but none of that matters now. I was hoping we could handle all of this amicably, but I see you could care less about my feelings. Goodbye, Aaron." She turned to leave.

She shouldn't have been surprised. Aaron had always been an asshole. She just hoped her children wouldn't turn out to be just like him.

Chapter 12

❧❧❧❧❧❧❧❧❧❧❧

Rachel Richards waited for Freya to arrive at the little bistro in the town square. She sat on the porch of the restaurant and sipped on her iced tea. The sun was out today and she soaked up its warmth.

Her friend had called in tears and Rachel had agreed to meet her. Rachel wondered why all of her friends seemed to be going through.

Rain had text them saying she'd left Derrick and no one had heard from her since. Prue had been off the grid, too, but Rachel just assumed she was working. Miranda seemed to be doing fine considering that her abusive husband was still missing. However, she seemed happy.

Rachel looked up and caught sight of Freya moving towards the restaurant. She waved her over and Freya approached the table. Rachel rose to her feet and hugged her friend.

Freya took a seat and removed her shades and then placed her purse in the chair at her side. Rachel noticed that her eyes were puffy—as if she'd been crying—but she didn't say anything.

"How was work?" Rachel asked.

Freya nodded. "It was fine. I'm still adjusting to being back in the working world."

Rachel simply nodded. She hadn't worked for a paycheck since she and Jack had gotten married. Volunteering had always been a choice for her. Now that Jack was dead, Rachel needed to find a new hobby. She couldn't just sit in that big empty house and drink all day.

Rachel sipped her iced tea as Freya flipped through the menu. She eyed her dear friend warily. "So, what's going on?"

Freya exhaled and placed her menu aside. "Short version or long version?"

Rachel moved her hair off her shoulder with a flick of the wrist. "Short version, I suppose."

Freya took a deep breath. "I'm pregnant with twins, I kicked Aaron out of the house, I filed for divorce, I served him with the papers myself, and he's having an affair with some slut at his job." She exhaled sharply and looked across the table. Rachel sat there—her face frozen in utter shock. "I know…it's a lot, right?" She reached for the glass of water that belonged to her dear friend and drank from it.

Rachel blinked and her jaw dropped. She cleared her throat and shook her head. "W-Well, first and foremost, I'm sorry. I know I should say congratulations, but I know you! You aren't excited about it."

"Thank you!" Freya exclaimed. She sighed heavily. "This shouldn't have happened."

"I thought Aaron got a vasectomy?"

"He didn't...He lied." Before Rachel could ask for the long version of her problems, Freya simply told her. She was in tears before she could finish.

Rachel rose from her seat and moved to hug her friend. A waitress neared the table. "Is everything alright?"

Rachel looked up. "Everything will be alright. She just needs a moment." The waitress nodded and moved away.

"I'm okay," Freya told Rachel and Rachel pulled away. Freya dabbed at her eyes with a napkin.

"I meant what I told the waitress. Everything *will* be alright."

"I'm not so sure, Rachel." She shook her head. "I don't know what I'm going to do with two more children. I mean, abortion is out of the question...I couldn't do that."

Rachel reached across the table and seized her best friend's hand. "I have your back, Freya. You aren't alone. I have that big old house. I can take the kids sometimes...Honestly, I could use the company. You're not alone, okay?"

Freya nodded. "You're the first person I've told outside of Aaron."

"Are you going to call your mother?"

Freya suddenly recalled what Aaron had said about her mother. Her heart broke. He'd changed on her instantly. "I probably will text her. She's going through so much." Freya looked around and saw the waitress coming. She was famished.

They quickly ordered and Freya eyed Rachel. Rachel had lost her husband not too long ago and though she still looked broken, she was beginning to look like her old self again.

Freya wondered how long it would be before she felt normal. Maybe she'd feel like herself once she gave birth to the twins.

Twins! She thought. She still couldn't believe it.

Their food soon arrived and Freya dug in—after all, she was eating for three now.

"Rachel…who was I after you met me?"

Rachel dabbed the corners of her mouth with her napkin and sat up straight. "Do you want the truth?"

"Always," Freya said.

"You changed, Freya. When I first met you, you were sassy and so full of life…You changed. You shrank to make room for Aaron."

Freya nodded in agreement. She couldn't even dispute the fact that she had changed. "I made room for Aaron and he took up the entire space. There wasn't any room left for me."

"Don't be too hard on yourself, Freya. We're *women*. We love fiercely and give up so much of ourselves for the men in our lives."

"I never asked for much."

"And perhaps that was part of the problem. Men only do what you allow. Trust me, I know. Jack ran things. I'd been taught how to take care of a man, but no one ever told me that a man was supposed to take care of his woman, too. Sure, they say give a man love and he'll put a roof over your head and clothes on your back. But there's so much more to it than that."

"I just wanted a partner who was loving and understanding. I wanted someone who wouldn't take advantage of me and would honor me. I just wanted Aaron to make an effort. He used to make me laugh, and now all he does is make me cry."

"Jack was the same way," Rachel said. "I loved him and I believe he might've loved me, too…but not completely. He never sacrificed for me."

"Aaron didn't either. He only took from me. He was never there when I needed him the most. He used to make me feel beautiful, and now…now all of that is over."

"Maybe you'll find love in the future?"

"How, Rae? *How*?! Who's going to love me with *seven* children?!" Tears began to well up again. "No man is going to look twice when he sees me pushing a double seater stroller, let alone with five kids—all under ten—in tow!" She sniffled and wiped her eyes. "I'll be all alone for the rest of my life."

Rachel shrugged. "At least you'll have children to keep you company. I'll die alone in that big house unless Jack's mistress and his bastard take it all from me."

Freya eyed Rachel with curiosity. And so, Rachel revealed to her pregnant friend about Robin Martez and her child.

Miranda laid in her bedroom with the lights off. She was balled into a fetal position and crying uncontrollably.

For years she'd allowed fear to dominate her life, but now she was free. George was dead. She didn't have to look over her shoulder and worry about Donatello. He wasn't coming after her anymore. She'd paid him off. That part of her life was over.

So why did she feel so guilty?

Miranda wiped her eyes and sat up. She brushed her hair away from her face and reached for her glasses. She forced herself out of bed and headed downstairs to tidy up the house.

But as she moved through the empty house—her child was at school—an emotion other than fear seemed to rise to the surface: anger.

Her pain came in waves, but so did her anger.

She was angry again as she moved through the house. She recalled the time George slammed her head into the wall. A dent still remained there.

She grew angrier as she headed through the living room. George had slapped her in the living room more than a dozen times. She grew furious as she raised her head and looked at the stairs. George had thrown her over the same banister he'd fallen over.

Miranda's house was filled with memories of abuse. It reeked of pain and suffering.

All through their marriage, Miranda had shrunk under George's control. She'd shut her feelings down to please him. She had doused her feelings in work and denial.

George used to make her doubt herself and used to make her feel dumb.

But guess who got the last laugh? *Miranda.*

"I killed him," she said aloud, her voice hoarse. "So, if I'm so free, why am I still so angry?"

She didn't know what to do with all of her anger. She closed her eyes and inhaled and then exhaled.

She tried to calm herself, but nothing seemed to help.

"I need to get out of this house," she told herself as she headed back upstairs to get dressed.

But where would she go?

Miranda removed her glasses and climbed into the shower and turned the dial until the warm water came shooting out of the nozzle. She moved under the spray and let the water caress her body.

Miranda closed her eyes and tried to relax.

"*Miranda,*" called an eerie voice.

Miranda dropped the bar of soap and spun around in the shower. She nearly lost her footing and fell. She felt a jolt of shock and her heart began to race. She knew that voice…she'd lived in fear under the thumb of that voice.

"*No,*" she groaned.

"*Miranda,*" called the voice again.

Miranda reached for the back scrubber in the corner of her shower and held it before her. "No!" she shouted. Steam filled the bathroom and she could barely see in front of her, but she knew this wasn't real; it couldn't be.

She reached down with one hand and turned the dial until the water stopped running, but she never took her eyes off the door to the shower.

Miranda tried to convince her pulse to slow as she climbed out of the shower. She quickly wrapped a towel around her body.

The eerie voice called her again and she spun around, steam passing over her flesh.

"Leave me alone," she whispered, fear gripping her. *He's dead.* "Leave me alone!" she shouted.

"Oh, I can't do that," said the voice of the spouse she'd murdered.

Miranda looked around but no one else was in the bathroom. She had to be going crazy. George was dead, he couldn't talk to her anymore.

She reached for the wide mirror and wiped steam off it. Miranda stared at her reflection and something caught her eye in the mirror.

She spun around and George's decomposed corpse appeared behind her. She screamed and fell backwards, knocking items over.

George stood before her, flesh falling off his face—blood pouring from the open wound in his temple.

Miranda crab walked backwards until her wet back was against the wall.

"You're dead!" she yelled, terrified.

"And *you* killed me," George's ghost said as he floated across the steam and neared Miranda.

She shook her head, fresh tears falling from her eyes. "No, no, no! This can't be happening."

"But it is, Miranda." The corpse chuckled. "You thought you could escape from me but you'll never be free of me, Miranda." He touched his chest. "I'm in *here*." Then he touched his bloody forehead and pressed a chubby finger to his temple. "And I'm in *here*."

Miranda was more afraid than she ever remembered.

"You took my life, Miranda! You'll never be rid of me."

"And what about MY life?!" she asked, forcing herself to her feet. "George, you deserved to die! You made my life a living hell!"

"But who said it was up to you to punish me?"

"And who told you it was okay to beat me?"

George's ghost took a step back. "I won't apologize for what I did."

Miranda looked away. The sight of George's ghost made her sick to her stomach. "I won't apologize for what I did, either. I guess we're both wrong."

She looked up, but George's ghost was gone.

Miranda quickly moved from the bathroom and headed to her bedroom. She needed to make a phone call. This was getting out of hand.

Now she was seeing her dead husband's ghost.

She found her cellphone and dialed a number, but it immediately went to voicemail.

Miranda sighed and waited to leave a message. "Hey, Rain. It's Miranda. I know you have a lot on your plate right now, but I need a huge favor...Can you help me put my house up for sale?"

Chapter 13

Rain was awakened by the buzzing of her cellphone. She looked at her cellphone and sent the call to voicemail. She hadn't slept well and being awakened by an unwanted call didn't help the situation. After telling Patty everything, Rain had cried her heart out.

Patty had helped her to the guest room that had once been Rain's bedroom and Rain had collapsed—exhausted.

Today, she forced herself to get out of bed. She prepared herself to read the first letter in the stack left behind by her father. Rain moved through the duplex and found Patty in the kitchen making breakfast.

She muttered a "*good morning*" and started to make coffee. The two women ate in silence and Patty kept eyeing Rain. Rain could feel her cousin's eyes on her, but she didn't want to talk about it anymore.

She'd told her cousin what Derrick had done and how he'd changed and how she wasn't so sure she wanted to be with him anymore. She wasn't even sure if she ever wanted to talk to him again.

Right now, she just wanted to focus on why she'd come to Liverpool in the first place.

"For what it's worth, I'm really glad you're home, Rain."

Rain sat her fork aside and grinned. "It feels nice to be back, too." She shrugged. "I might stay for good. Who knows?"

"Are you sure you want to leave him?"

Rain shrugged and finished her food. "I'm going to open a letter."

"Do you mind if I sit with you?"

Rain nodded. "I could use the company."

The two women settled on the couch in the living room and Rain pulled the stack of letters from the trunk and lifted the first one to eye level.

Rain opened the envelope and pulled out a sheet of paper covered in her father's handwriting.

'*To my precious Rain,*

There is so much that I want to tell you. There's so much that I want to share with you. I wish I had more time. I wish the family had more time.

You are my greatest accomplishment, Rain. I hate that I never told you the truth. I'm dying baby and if you're reading this letter then I've passed on.

I'm sorry you had to find out this way. I just wasn't strong enough to ever come out and say it. I have colon cancer and it's been pretty aggressive. I'm sure you've noticed me getting sicker and thinner.

But I've been lying to myself and saying you haven't noticed.

So, to compensate for the words I can't say, I'm going to write them. I want you to be able to have something of mine when I'm gone.

These letters will serve as our last conversations. These are conversations I wish I would've been man enough to tell you in person.

Please forgive me, Rain, for being a stubborn man. Your mother and I agreed that this was best.

I've tried my best to shield you from all of this pain. I want you to hold your innocence for a little while longer.

I'm fighting, Rain. I really am, but I feel like I'm losing this battle.

I want to take this time to start writing you letters telling you everything. I want you to know that I love you.

I will most likely miss every important day in your life and I'm sorry for that. I'm sorry that I can't stop you from feeling the pain of my death.

I'm going to miss the first time you drive a car and get your license. I'm going to miss your prom and high school graduation. I'm going to miss you graduating from college.

I'm going to miss seeing you fall in love for the first time and I'm going to miss threatening the young man that comes to my door to pick you up.

I'm going to miss you growing up and I'm so, so sorry.

I wish I could be there for when you get married one day.

I wish I could meet the man that will one day have the privilege of having you in his life. I wish I could be there to walk you down the aisle someday.

But if I just so happen to leave this world before then, I'll be there with you in spirit.

Love,

Daddy

Tears fell on the paper, soaking the ink, and Rain realized that she'd been crying. She sniffled and wiped her eyes.

"I never knew he had cancer," she told her cousin.

Patty hugged her. "Neither did I." She sighed. "Uncle Rick was a great man, Rain."

"I just wish we'd had more time."

"So did he, sweetie," her cousin said, reassuring her. Rain rose from the couch and went to the bathroom.

Patty reached for her cordless landline phone and then grabbed Rain's cellphone. The device lay on the end table before her. She scrolled through Rain's contacts and found the number she'd been looking for.

She pressed the phone to her ear as it rang. Finally, a voice answered on the other end. Patty cleared her throat. "Hey, this is Patty. I'm not sure if you remember me or not, but I just had to call…Your wife needs you. She needs you more than she knows…"

Overseas, Derrick moved through the condominium. "Is she alright? Where are you? She hasn't returned any of my calls or texts." Derrick had no idea what was wrong with Rain.

He'd been going through so much. Between cutting things off with Donatello and still looking over his shoulder in case his goons came after him and then moving to New York and starting at a new label, Derrick felt stressed beyond reason. Rain had been there. She was his and he'd only taken what was already his.

He'd been so enticed by her that he'd wanted her right then and there.

And then she'd left with no warning. He thought something had happened to her. He'd been worried about her. New York was a city filled with crazies. Anything could've happened.

Sure, they'd had a bit of rough sex but he didn't think that warranted her ghosting him.

However, a few days ago he'd come home and caught sight of her rings on the counter and a few of her things were missing, too.

Derrick sighed heavily and ran a hand over his face. "She left me, didn't she?" he asked, a hint of pain in his voice.

"Yes, she did. How could you?"

"How could I what?" he asked, lowering his voice despite the fact that he was the only person in the condominium.

"You know what you did to her."

"I don't see how that's any of your business. What goes on between me and my wife is our business. Respect that."

Patty sighed. "I didn't call to argue. Rain needs you right now...She's going through a lot."

"Where is she?"

"Sh-She's staying with me back at the family home."

Derrick sucked in a breath. "She's in the UK?" *She's gone for real.* "I can't lose her, Patty. Stop her. Don't let her leave. I'm coming."

Chapter 14

Prue popped several sleeping pills and climbed into her big empty bed. She was back on Lyfe Road in her brown Craftsman styled home. She just wanted to sleep her pain away. Yes, she would sleep and no longer have to deal with Romeo's betrayal.

Donatello had yet to return her calls and she didn't expect him to at this point. Their marriage was over.

She suddenly felt hopelessly depressed again as she climbed into bed. Her doctor had called back saying that she could see Prue back in the office in nine business days.

Prue had wanted to start antiretroviral treatment as soon as possible, but that didn't seem to be an option. It would take some time. Her doctor had told her that when Prue came into the office they'd draw some blood for a CD4 count test which would look at how many CD4 cells were in a small amount of blood.

Prue had learned from the internet that the CD4 cells, also called T-helper cells, were an important part of her immune system because their job was to fight infections and germs. HIV attacked those T cells and reduced those cells in the body.

Prue knew from TV and movies that without treatment it would be harder for her body to fight off the illness. She'd decided that she wanted to fight for her life.

Even though she'd see her doctor in nine days, Prue wondered how long it would be before she'd start a pill regimen.

For once in her adult life, she'd chosen herself. But first she needed to sleep. She needed to drift off into nothingness.

As Prue rolled over, she suddenly had a desire to talk to her mother. She hadn't talked to Vivian Sanchez in months. The last time she'd tried to call her mother, the woman hadn't answered.

Prue grabbed her phone and scrolled through her contacts and stopped at '*Vivian.*' Prue sighed and pressed the call button.

Surprisingly, Vivian Sanchez picked up on the second ring. "Prudence, what a surprise!" her mother exclaimed. "I've been meaning to call you back. You know we've been so busy getting your little sister ready for her little soiree."

Prue had to smile despite herself. "She's getting married, Ma."

"Well, I'm trying to be happy so calling it a soiree makes me feel better."

Prue sat up in her bed and listened as her mom began to dive into wedding details. Prue felt her chest tighten as she tried to get a word in.

"Ma…" Prue said, but still Vivian went on and on, complaining about the lack of a budget. She was furious that she'd only been allotted $800 for the reception. "Mama…"

Suddenly, Vivian stopped talking and Prudence knew that her mother had finally heard her. "Prudence…what's wrong, hija?"

Prue felt a cluster of emotions explode out of her and she began to cry. She sniffled and wiped her eyes, but the tears kept coming.

Concern filled Vivian's voice for the first time in a long time. "Prue tell me. What's wrong, baby? You can tell mama. Where are you?"

"I'm home, Ma. I'm here."

"Is Donatello there? Did he hurt you?"

Prue exhaled sharply. "There's just so much going on, Ma. I don't know what I'm doing anymore."

"Baby, life is hard. I know it can seem like you're alone, but you're not. You have a man that loves you—"

"I don't, Ma. Donatello is hardly ever home. He doesn't love me anymore."

Vivian was silent for a moment. "Even *if* he doesn't love you anymore, *I* love you. I love you, Prudence, no matter what."

"I know, Ma. I know you love me, but sometimes a woman just needs someone besides her mother to love her."

"You have a point there." Vivian Sanchez chuckled slightly. Prue could hear noise in the background and assumed it was her sisters. "Do you want to talk about it?"

"Yes, but not over the phone."

"When are you coming down? You know the wedding is—"

"Mom…I need you."

"I'm here, Prue. Just tell me what's really going on. What kind of problems are the two of you having?"

"Mom," Prue repeated. "I need you."

There was silence on the other end for a moment and Prue wondered if her mother was still there. She looked at her phone and sure enough, the line was still open. She was surprised that they'd been on the phone longer than five minutes.

Finally, Vivian spoke. "I'll be there tomorrow."

Prue's heart swelled with love. "Really?"

"You sound so shocked!" exclaimed Vivian. Truth be told, Prue was shocked. "Should I bring your sisters?"

"No. I'll shoot them a text so they won't worry, but right now I just need my mom."

"Okay, baby…I'll be there as soon as possible."

Across the pond, Rain placed the second letter to the side. She still couldn't believe that her parents had hid her father's illness from her. However, this second letter had broken her down even more.

In this letter Rain's father, Rick, told her what to look for in a mate. He'd left her a detailed list of red flags and Rain couldn't believe that a lot of the red flags were things that Derrick constantly did.

The doorbell rang and she heard footsteps behind her and turned to see Patty racing to answer the door. "I'll get it!" shouted Patty.

Rain shrugged and returned to the trunk. She heard the door open and close and eased herself onto the couch. She reached for the third letter.

"Hello, Rain," came a voice from behind her.

She froze and turned to find Derrick in the doorway standing next to Patty.

Rain jumped to her feet. "What's going on? Wh-What are you doing here?!" She looked at her cousin. "What did you do?"

Patty's eyes widened. "I just wanted—"

Derrick held up a hand to stop her. He kept his eyes on his wife. "Patty, would you excuse us, please? I'd like to have a moment alone with my wife."

Patty turned to leave and Rain's breath hitched. "Patty?"

Patty stopped and looked at Rain then to Derrick. "I'll be in the next room." She eyed Rain and mouthed '*it's okay.*'

But it wasn't. Patty had betrayed her. Seeing Derrick was the last thing she had wanted.

Why didn't Patty know that?! She'd told her cousin what had happened. Why had she revealed to Derrick where she was?

Derrick took a step towards Rain and she took a step back. He held up a hand and halted. "Whoa, whoa. What's wrong with you, Rain? Why are you acting like I hit you or something? I've been worried out of my mind for—"

"You should leave," she told him. She was beyond uncomfortable. This was wrong.

"Rain, please…can we just talk?"

"The time to talk was before you did what you did."

Derrick took a deep breath and placed a hand over his mouth. "Rain, I think you misunderstood what happened. Perhaps your brain twisted the images of reality…"

She frowned and her lips twisted in agitation. "Are you kidding me?! What the hell is wrong with you, Derrick? So, you think I imagined you pressing me against the window and lifting my dress? You think I imagined you pinning me there while you—"

She had to stop, she couldn't say it. She placed a hand over her mouth and glanced at him. He simply stood there and she froze in horror. Who was this man before her? He wasn't her husband.

This was a stranger.

"I've been in pain for days, Rain! I was worried about you. I thought New York had swallowed you up and spit you out. I thought you'd been harmed."

"It's getting harder to pretend that I'm not pissed off. Derrick you—"

"It's like I've been living with a ghost for months and then you just up and left."

Rain shut her mouth and stood there. She agreed that things had changed. Derrick felt like a ghost, too. It was like she didn't even know him. "There's nothing about what happened that is forgivable. This side of you is something I've never seen before. What's got you acting so brand new?"

"Damn, I'm so confused." He began to pace back and forth. "You think I've flipped the script and I feel the same. You changed, Rain."

"No, *you* shut me out and then you dragged me across the country! You didn't even—"

"Ah! Here we go! I was wondering when you'd play the victim, like I forced you to be in a situation you didn't want to be in."

"This just isn't you. I mean you look the same, but I don't know you at all. And *yes*…you did force me into something I never wanted to happen. Derrick, you *hurt me*." She felt her eyes grow moist but she refused to cry. Flashes of the rape filled her mind and she tried to shake the memories away.

"Let's just both calm down and talk this through. Let's just put everything on the table."

"I don't want to talk, Derrick. I just realized that for over two years I've been living with a stranger."

"I miss you, Rain…I hate the distance between us. Just come home."

She looked at him—dazed and confused. Was he not hearing her? Was she not clear?

"You can stop pushing me away. I'm not giving up on us."

"Let me be perfectly clear, Derrick…I'm not coming back to that condo. I don't want to see you ever again. I don't want anything to do with you. You RAPED me and—"

"That's a lie!" he shouted and she recoiled. "We made love and then you just left."

"Were we not in the same room?! How many times did I say 'stop' and 'no', Derrick? You ignored me! You forced yourself on me! You don't do that to somebody you love!"

"We're not calling it quits on our marriage, Rain. Divorce isn't an option. I don't want us to end up like your friends."

She frowned. "What does that mean?" She shook her head. "It's neither here nor there. I don't care. It's over, Derrick."

He stood there and simply stared at her. This conversation wasn't going anywhere.

"I'll do whatever it takes to get you to come home…Home is where you belong."

"You need help, Derrick…serious help."

His head snapped up and he glared at her. "You've got me all the way fucked up."

That was when Rain knew she'd crossed a line. She'd never been fearful of Derrick until the attack. But as she looked across the living room at her husband, she understood that she was fearful now.

Rain didn't realize that she'd been backing up until she felt the ottoman hit the back of her legs.

"You were a pathetic *sales* associate who could barely afford her college tuition when I met you. You were a loner and an orphan and nobody wanted you. *I* loved you. I took you in and gave you a family. I welcomed you into my world and gave you a life you could be proud of."

"Derrick, just—"

He scoffed. "You ungrateful bitch."

And at that exact moment, Patty walked back into the room. "Okay, Derrick, you need to leave."

He looked at her and Patty stopped in her tracks. He glared at her and then turned his eyes on Rain. "Do you know how many women would kill to be married to me? I'm a music producer! I make dreams come true! Do you know how many women have tried to get a man like me and live in the fancy condo I bought? Hell, even the house I bought for you on Lyfe Road should have been enough to keep a simple bitch like you content! I gave you *everything!*"

Patty moved to intersept Derrick as he moved towards Rain, but Rain gestured for her to stop.

Adrenaline pumped through Rain's body. She needed to get him to calm down. She needed to call the police. She needed to get away.

"You're right, Derrick," she said and Patty looked at her, shocked. She wished her cousin would call the police! Why was she still here? What did Patty think she could do if Derrick lashed out?

"You aren't even worth the trouble you put me through." He moved towards her and Patty crossed the room and grabbed his arm.

"Derrick, you need to leave!" yelled Patty.

Derrick threw her aside and Patty fell to the ground. Rain moved towards her cousin but Derrick seized her by the throat and she gasped.

"You're so fucking problematic! You black bitches never appreciate a black king! Do you know what I've done for you!?" Derrick thought of all Donatello had put him through. Memories of dark deeds flashed across his mind as he wrapped his hands around Rain's throat and began to squeeze.

Rain tried to get his hands off her as Patty hit Derrick with her little hands and tried to pull him off her cousin.

"You were supposed to love me forever."

"I do love you!" Rain lied, wheezing as he shoved his fingers into her windpipe. Rain gasped and kicked at Derrick, but he was too strong for her.

Rain suddenly felt light headed and realized she was running short on oxygen. She was glad Patty had been here to see Derrick's transformation into a madman. She'd never be able to explain the violence otherwise.

However, Rain had hoped that he would halt his attack once Patty had gotten involved, but that hadn't happened.

It was almost like he'd come after her in a blind rage.

Rain's windpipe felt as if it was being crushed and the pain was overwhelming. Her lungs were burning and she tried to push Derrick's face.

At that moment, he slammed her head into the wall.

"I fucking hate you," he told her, his voice soft. And those were the last words Rain heard before she blacked out.

Derrick released her and she slid to the floor in a heap. Patty screamed and dropped to her knees.

"You crazy fuck!" Patty shouted.

"This is on you," he told her. Patty looked away as she tried to rouse her cousin.

Derrick had stolen for Donatello, hidden drugs, and committed attempted murder for the man, too. He'd done so much more in the name of fame. And now Rain was trying to bring him down.

He adjusted his clothes and ran a hand over his close-cropped hair.

It was at this moment that Derrick realized he was turning into George Copeland.

No, I AM George, he thought to himself. He looked at his hands and then to his unconscious wife.

"What have I done?" he asked himself in a small voice.

"Get the hell out of here!" Patty shouted.

Rain awoke in a hospital bed. Her throat felt raw and she was thirsty. Her vision was spotty and she had a sickening headache.

After a while, she moved—fear had immobilized her and she hadn't wanted to move in case Derrick was here. But the second she moved, Patty moved to her side and filled her vision.

"Rain, I'm so, so, sorry! I-I didn't know—"

"I—" Rain cringed at the pain she felt in her throat and she cleared her throat. "Water," she whispered and Patty quickly fetched her a cup of lukewarm water.

"Rain, I had no idea he was abusive."

"He didn't use to be…This is new," she told her cousin after she had a drink. "I can't believe you called and told him where I was. How could you?"

"I thought he was a good man, Rain! I-I had no idea."

"You should've listened to me when I told you that I never wanted to see him again. What, did you think I was lying when I told you he raped me?" Patty shook her head. Rain rolled her eyes and shifted in the stiff bed until her back was to her cousin. "Just leave, please."

Derrick could've killed her. She was just glad that he hadn't. Even though Patty was the reason she was in the hospital now, Rain realized that she shouldn't take her anger out on Patty. She looked over her shoulder and caught sight of her younger cousin sitting in a chair. The woman was silently crying.

Patty looked up and realized her cousin was looking at her. "After you blacked out, he apologized for shoving me. He said that he was upset and shouldn't have done that, but you'd 'gone too far'," Patty told her, using rabbit ears when she said 'gone too far.'

Rain exhaled. "I don't know what to do."

"You need to get out of here," Patty told her. "You need to go to the authorities. You need to—"

"I thought I was safe here." She saw a pained expression on Patty's face but couldn't be concerned with that. "I don't know what to do. I have nowhere else to go."

"Lyfe Road?" asked Patty. "You have friends there."

Rain shook her head. "That's too predictable. If I leave here, he'll know to look there next."

Patty reached out and took Rain's hand. "We'll figure it out. I promise, I won't fail you again."

Rain squeezed Patty's hand and then released it. "Derrick used to seem so perfect…It seemed like overnight the person I loved just vanished."

"How could a man like that become a monster?" asked Patty, her voice filled with surprise and confusion.

Rain wondered the same thing. *What on Earth changed my husband?*

Chapter 15

Prudence had welcomed her mother into her home, but after revealing to her mother the truth about her life, Vivian Sanchez had decided to stay at a nearby hotel instead. Prue couldn't blame her mom. She'd revealed a lot.

She'd been open and honest about her affair with Romeo and subsequently contracting HIV. She'd omitted the part of her story that involved Donatello shooting Romeo.

Vivian had been overwhelmed and couldn't believe what Prue had done. She hadn't raised a daughter to be unfaithful. She hadn't raised a daughter who didn't love herself, and to Vivian it was apparent that Prue didn't love herself.

Prue simply laid in bed, unable to move. She didn't feel well and she was running a fever. She simply assumed that stress was getting the best of her.

She heard a door open and close and assumed it was her mother with her dinner—she'd borrowed Prue's car to go to a nearby restaurant for take-out. However, when she heard heavy footsteps on the stairs, she realized it wasn't her mother.

She rolled over and caught sight of Donatello in the door way. She instantly sat up. "Donny!"

"What are you doing here?" he asked, his voice cold.

"I live here," she answered, perplexed.

"I didn't know you were here. I didn't see your car outside."

"Ma has my car. She went to go pick up dinner."

"Ah," he said. "It's good you called your mother. I'm sure she's glad our marriage is over. Is she helping you move out, too?"

"What?" she asked. "What made you think I was moving out?"

He looked at her and frowned. "You thought you were going to get the house if we split up? Prue, get serious. I bought this house and once I file for divorce I'm selling it."

Prudence threw back the comforter. She climbed out of bed and stomped across the master bedroom. "So, you're just going to kick me out?"

"Well if we're splitting, you can't stay here, Prue. Let's be reasonable. Once we get a divorce, I can move to New York full-time. There's no need to—"

"I can't believe you'd do that."

"You have your own money, Prue. There's no reason for you to stay here, beyond your friends."

She shook her head. She didn't want to fight. She didn't have it in her. She simply wanted to lay down. Her head throbbed with a migraine forming and she needed silence. "Okay, Donatello. I really don't want to fight. Whatever you want to do is fine by me."

He was taken aback by her surrender. He wasn't expecting her to give up so easily. "Well we have a prenup in place and no children, so it should go by smoothly. You cheated on me, Prudence, and got caught. There's no coming back from that."

"For what it's worth, I'm sorry…"

Donatello looked at her and frowned. "Prue, are you feeling okay? You look awfully pale."

She rubbed her forehead and realized she was perspiring. "I feel like crap." She turned towards the bed and her eyes fluttered. Seconds later, she collapsed.

"Prue!" Donatello shouted and he rushed to her side. "Prue!"

———————————

It was all over the news. There were lies and assumptions about why the famed Supermodel Prudence Cameron was in the hospital.

Some tabloids said she'd overdosed while another outlet said she was caught snorting coke in a club. Yet another news outlet had been told by a 'credible source' that she'd collapsed backstage at a fashion show.

However, none of the assumptions were true. But with Prue refusing to release any type of public statement—much to her publicist's frustration—no one was really sure of what had actually happened to land her in the hospital.

But *Prue* knew why she was in the hospital. She was still struggling with coming to terms with her condition and it was beginning to get the best of her.

After Donatello excused himself from the hospital room, the ER doctor reminded Prudence that having HIV wasn't a death sentence. But Prue felt otherwise. She was losing everything.

"Have you told your husband?" the doctor asked. Prue looked at the older woman and the doctor nodded. "You should tell him. We're legally obligated to inform your partner, but personally I've learned that it's better if it comes from you."

Prue sighed heavily. "The person who infected me didn't even tell me…"

"Is that what you want to do to your husband, too?" asked the doctor.

Prue realized that she'd been doing that anyway without even realizing it. She bit her lower lip and the doctor nodded.

"You're feeling a ton of emotions, Mrs. Cameron, but you need to get ahead of this. A woman of your position should especially get ahead of this."

"My name is splashed across the tabloids," Prue told her. "I just know Donatello…We're already getting a divorce. I don't want to make it worse."

"Withholding your status from a partner and putting them at risk is illegal. I won't tell you how to feel, but from a medical perspective, you need to tell your husband. You said it yourself that you're already getting divorced. Tell him…if you don't you might end up in jail." And with that, the doctor left the room. Prue relaxed into her pillow and wondered where Romeo was.

She'd been thinking about him nonstop—but not for the reasons one would assume—and knew that she needed to talk to him. But the doctor was right. She needed to talk to Donatello, too.

Prue's mother had stepped out of the room twenty minutes ago to call Prue's sisters. She wondered when she'd be back.

The hospital door opened and Donatello stepped back in. "I called your friends. Rain didn't answer, but the others are on the way."

"Thank you, Donatello…for everything. You didn't even have to stay with me, but you did. That means a lot."

"Just because our marriage didn't work out doesn't mean I don't care about you," he told her as he took a seat next to her bed side. "So, are the doctors saying what's wrong? Is it exhaustion?"

Prue shook her head and he nodded and relaxed in his seat.

"Well, I'll stay for a little while longer then I need to head to the airport."

Despite the closeness of Donatello sitting at her bedside, Prue had never felt so far away from him. With every second that passed, Prue felt him withdrawing from her—the connection between then was dissolving.

Prue found herself shrinking into her hospital bed, away from him, mimicking the distance she felt between them.

All the warmth that had been there in the beginning of their marriage was gone now.

Prue pulled the thin hospital cover around her shoulder and tried to sit up.

Donatello hadn't left her side since he'd brought her to the hospital, but he seemed to be elsewhere entirely. He wasn't with her mentally. Prue wondered what he was thinking about.

Prue's pulse quickened as she turned towards him. Everything was about to change…again. "We need to talk," she whispered.

Donatello peeled his eyes from his phone screen and eyed her. "I was just thinking the same thing. I thought maybe you had the flu but—"

"That's what we need to talk about." She lifted her chin and stared at her husband. "The next time you're having a terrible day, here's something to keep in mind: you've probably got it better than Prudence."

He put his phone down and sat up straight. "I'm listening."

"Whether you believe it or not, I *do* respect you, Donatello, and I don't want you to hear it from someone else."

He swallowed. "You're pregnant, aren't you?" he asked. Prue sucked in a breath. "And let me guess, it's not mine?" He pressed his lips into a thin line and Prue noticed that he clenched his jaw.

She shook her head. "N-No…that's not it. I'm not pregnant."

Donatello sighed in relief and ran a hand through his growing hair. "So, what is it?"

"Donny…" Prue suddenly felt a lump rise in her throat. It was now or never. "I'm HIV positive."

Donny simply stared at her for what seemed like forever. His lips moved slightly but there was no sound. He sat there, cleared his throat, tried to talk, and yet nothing came out.

"Donny?" Prue called out. Her cheeks felt warm and she reached up to touch her face. She felt tears on the back of her hand and realized that she'd started crying.

She was terrified of revealing this to him.

Donatello shakily rose to his feet. He blinked, exhaled sharply, and turned away from her.

"Please, don't go," Prue pleaded, her voice shaking.

Donatello slightly turned. "How long have you known?'" he asked, his voice devoid of emotion.

"Not long," she admitted. "I still don't even know what to think about it."

He nodded slightly and rubbed his forehead. "Well, you cheated on me…This is your karma." Prudence gasped. He shook his head. "I want you out of my house before the end of the week."

"Donatello, please! You don't understand—"

He whirled around to face her. "Oh, I understand! You fucked around and got the package, Prue! It's only what you deserve! But so help me God, if I have it, I'll kill you!"

Prue recoiled from his words and her breath hitched. "I never meant for any of this to happen."

Donatello kicked over a chair and Prue yelped. He swore and knocked over several items in the room. "When I shot that little prick, I should've shot you, too!"

"Donny, I—"

The door to the room opened and Vivian Sanchez rushed into the room, followed by a nurse.

"Is everything alright in here?" the nurse asked.

Vivian looked at her daughter then at the items scattered across the floor. "Did he hit you?" she asked. Prue shook her head. Vivian looked at Donatello. "Perhaps you should leave."

"I'll call security," said the nurse.

Donatello held up his hand. "There's no need. I'm leaving." He headed towards the door and Vivian moved to pull her daughter into her arms. Before he left the hospital room, Donatello turned to face Prue. "If it wasn't clear before, let me make it clear now…We're *over*. I'm filing for divorce today."

"Can she at least get her things?" Vivian asked.

Donatello ignored his mother-in-law's question and glared at Prudence. "You're dead to me."

Prue burst into tears and her mother patted her back and let her sob in her bosom.

"How'd you get yourself into this mess?" Vivian asked.

"Mother, I can't take you judging me right now!" Prue wailed. A knock sounded at the door and Vivian looked up.

"Go away," the older woman said. But the door opened anyway.

Prue pulled away from her mother and discovered that three of her best friends stood there—Rachel in red, Miranda in black, and Freya in brown.

Prue smiled through her tears and extended her arms towards them. "Oh, I'm so glad you're here."

The three women moved into the room and made a beeline to Prudence.

Vivian stepped aside as Miranda crushed Prudence in a hug. Rachel hugged Mrs. Sanchez and Freya waited for her turn.

"How are you?" Miranda asked, taking a seat on Prue's hospital bed.

"I'm a mess," Prue replied.

"We see," said Rachel, grimacing. Prue chuckled and sniffled then wiped her eyes.

Freya eyed Mrs. Sanchez. "Why is she crying?"

Vivian eyed her daughter and was about to speak, but Prue beat her to it. "Donny just left. It's over…for real this time."

The women began to all talk at once, but Vivian stopped them. "She's had a very stressful day and is still regaining her strength. She needs her rest. Perhaps you should come back later?"

Rachel was about to mutter a rebuttal when there was another knock at the door. The five women in the room turned towards the door.

A second later, the door opened and a man walked in dressed in jeans and a designer shirt.

"What are **you** doing here?" Miranda asked, rising to her feet. She blocked Prue's view, but by Miranda's tone, Prue instantly knew who it was.

"Leave, young man!" Vivian said, walking towards Romeo Lupe'. "You've already caused enough problems."

"Please, ma'am. I just want to talk to Prue," Romeo said with a thick French accent.

"That's not going to happen today!" exclaimed Vivian. "I have a few choice words for you!"

"Ma," said Prue, a warning in her voice. Vivian looked at her eldest daughter and Prue nodded. Vivian exhaled sharply and then turned to glare at Romeo.

"Your ass is grass," sneered Vivian and then she shoved past him as she walked out of the room.

Miranda eyed Prue and Prue nudged her head towards the door. Miranda caught the hint. Prue wanted to talk to him alone.

Miranda touched Rachel's shoulder as she passed her and the other women from Lyfe Road vacated the hospital room and moved into the hall.

As the door closed, Romeo turned to Prue—a bouquet of roses in his hands.

"What are you doing here?" Prue asked, crossing her arms over her chest.

She'd had a long day and she was too emotionally drained to deal with Romeo's BS.

"I'm sorry, Prue. I was wrong. I know you will never forgive me, but—"

"I've lost everything…my husband, my home…"

"You still have your friends…they're here for you. And you still have me."

"I can't even believe you'd say something like that."

"Prue, I love you. It was a mistake not to tell you. I was afraid you'd think I was tainted and unworthy of your love."

"You were unworthy of *me,*" she replied. "Romeo, you took away my options. You played Russian roulette with my life and I lost. There's no coming back from that."

He placed the roses on the end of the bed. "Prudence, I know you'll never forgive me in this life, but—"

"Please, just go." She looked away, forcing her eyes to focus on the window. "I'm exhausted and I can't do this right now."

"I'll be in the lobby, Prue. I came as soon as I heard and I'm not going anywhere."

"I thought maybe you were coming to give me a real apology, but no. You're just coming with more excuses." She exhaled sharply but refused to look at him. "I told Donatello the truth."

Romeo was silent for a moment as the effects of her words soaked in. "So…it's over for you two then?"

Finally, Prue looked at him. "Is that what you wanted? You wanted Donatello to leave me? Is that why you had unprotected sex with me and gave me HIV?"

"I always only wanted you, Prue. It was always you."

She scoffed. "Just by any means necessary, right?" She shook her head and frowned. "How can you even say that when you're gay—well, *bisexual,* as you claim?"

"I'm bi, Prue. It's possible for me to love you because I like men *and* women. I've never felt this strongly towards a woman before and—"

"And that's why you decided to give me your ultimate gift?" She glared at him. "You're a poisoned apple, Romeo, and I picked you off the Tree of Knowledge."

"I am **not** poison, Prue! I've allowed you to bash me long enough, but I'm still human! I still deserve respect and—"

She rolled her eyes. "You lost my respect when you lied to me." She sighed heavily. "Please, just go. I'll call you when I'm ready to talk."

Prue shifted in her hospital bed and turned with her back facing Romeo. She glanced out the window and watched as day turned to night.

Romeo sunk to the floor and never left her side.

Chapter 16

Across the pond, Rain was released from the hospital and appalled to find Derrick was waiting for her when Patty wheeled her through the exit.

"You can't do this, Derrick," said Patty. "She doesn't want to see you!"

Rain looked at the man who was and was not a mystery to her. Derrick stood before her dressed in dark jeans and a plain blue shirt. Dark stubble lined his jaw and he appeared tired—as if he hadn't slept since she'd been in the hospital.

He appeared perfectly normal to her, but she knew that there was a beast inside of him that threatened her well-being.

As Patty tried to move past him and wheel Rain to her car, thoughts of their past flashed before Rain's mind's eye.

She saw her husband on their wedding day. He looked so handsome in a tuxedo.

She saw her husband holding her on their honeymoon.

Then, she saw the monster that had not only raped her but had tried to kill her as well.

"I'm sorry, Rain," he said, trying to move towards her. "Please, I just want to talk. Is there any possibility that you'll give me another chance?"

Patty tried to steer Rain away from Derrick. Patty scowled at Derrick. "Derrick, I think it's time for you to leave. Stop doing this. She doesn't want to see you. Haven't you done enough?"

Rain looked over her shoulder as Patty led her away. "Goodbye, Derrick." And they moved away from the man that had loved and hurt her.

Rachel Richards was beginning to feel like her old self again. She'd booked a spa day and had plans to meet Freya and Miranda for a day of relaxation. As she pulled on a yellow blouse and jeans, she reached for her cellphone and called Prue to check on her.

Prue was being released today and she wanted to make sure she'd be okay. Rachel had agreed to let Prue stay with her until she was able to find a new place.

She couldn't believe that Donatello had only given her a few days to pack up her entire life and get out.

What on Earth was going on?

Everyone's lives were in shambles. Freya was pregnant and divorcing her man, Rain had left her man and ran off to the UK, Miranda's crazy husband was still missing, and now Prue was getting kicked out of her home and Donatello had filed for divorce.

She couldn't believe that all their lives had changed so drastically in such a short time.

Rachel pulled her red hair into a ponytail and began to search for her car keys as she ended the call with Prue. She was trying to put her life back together the best way she knew how.

Sure, Jack was gone now and things were different, but she had to keep on living. She'd yet to clear out his side of the closet or empty his drawers from the dresser. He was gone but she wasn't ready to let go just yet.

Baby steps, she told herself as she headed to the front door. She opened the front door and stepped out. Rachel locked the door and turned to head towards her car but stopped.

Her face twisted in dismay as she caught sight of a woman heading up her walkway.

"Mrs. Richards, I'm glad I caught you!" said Robin Martez.

Rachel exhaled in agitation and moved to the edge of her porch. "Well, there goes my day," Rachel said aloud.

Her entire countenance shifted as Robin approached her.

"Were you on your way out?" asked Robin.

Rachel grinned but the gesture lacked kindness. "As a matter of fact, yes. I was headed out to enjoy my day." Rachel tried to move beyond the woman, but Robin placed a hand on Rachel's forearm. Rachel froze and then looked at the woman's hand.

Robin withdrew her hand and took a step back. "Can I just have a moment of your time?"

"The moment has passed," Rachel said and moved down the walkway and to her car.

Robin quickly caught up. "I just wanted you to meet someone." Rachel skidded to a stop and Robin moved to her car.

Rachel swallowed hard. She knew *exactly* who Robin wanted her to meet. Robin opened the back door of her car and helped a small child out of the car.

The child reached for Robin's hand and they walked back up the driveway until they stood directly in front of Rachel.

Rachel couldn't breathe. The child wore a pink dress and her dark hair was in pigtails.

Robin grinned down at the child but composed herself as she looked at Rachel. "I'd like to introduce you to my daughter." She looked at the child. "Maria, say hello to Mrs. Richards."

The little girl waved. Rachel's heart sank. Maria' eyes pierced Rachel's soul…They were *Jack's* eyes.

"Rachel?" called Robin, pulling Rachel from her thoughts.

Rachel knelt before the child before she'd even realized what she was doing. The little girl grinned at Rachel. "Well, hello there, Maria. Aren't you just the prettiest little thing?"

"Thank you," the child said shyly, hiding behind her mother.

Rachel rose to her full height and sighed heavily. She looked Robin square in the eyes. "I'd like a paternity test."

Rachel was late to her spa day with the girls, but this was more important. She raced across town, driving much faster than she should have.

With haste, Rachel drove to Jack's grave only accompanied by the sound of her sobs. Meeting little Maria had hurt her more than she'd imagined.

Rachel pulled up to the grave and finally slowed as she pulled up to a dirt patch near where Jack's headstone was. Balloons and flowers adorned his grave, most likely left by fans. Rachel had to remember that they were grieving, too.

She moved to stand at his headstone. Despite her attempt to stop crying, she couldn't. Her heart was still attached to Jack even after his death. She'd thought she'd severed those ties, but clearly she was wrong.

With every new hurt she felt the band-aid on her heart was ripped off. She felt anger roiling off her in waves.

She was angry because he'd left her. She was angry because he'd lied. He'd left her all alone in a house that was much too big for just one person. He'd left her in a bed meant for two.

Jack had broken her heart long before she'd found out he had Hepatitis C. And when she'd found out that he'd not only had yet another affair, but had also fathered a child, Rachel found the tiny fragments that represented the remains of her heart broken into even smaller pieces.

Even from the grave Jack was causing her pain and tormenting her. She felt as if the broken record was playing again.

Robin had given Jack the one thing Rachel had never been able to give him: a child. And according to Robin, Jack had continued to provide for them and had spent time with them. Was it the truth? Was it a lie?

Rachel wished she could ask Jack.

She wished she could look into his eyes and see the truth or catch him in a lie. But that wasn't an option.

There was no more time for questions. Now she just needed a solution.

She stood before his headstone filled with anger, hurt, and betrayal and released it all. She screamed and fell to her knees—her sobs echoed off the ground and filled the air.

"How could you do this to me?!" she shouted, slamming her fist into the soft earth before her. "I could've sworn we were in love! I gave you my heart! And yet, here I am, standing here all by myself. I devoted my *life* to you and gave you the best years of my life, and this is how you repay me?! Huh?" She crawled towards his headstone and slapped her palms against it. "Huh, Jack? You die and leave some *whore* behind with your bastard?"

Rachel shook her head. She was sure she looked like a crazy woman, but she didn't care.

"Once again I feel like a fool because of you! I tried my best to make our marriage work, but I was never enough for you! Why was I not enough for you?!"

Rachel felt herself coming undone and wondered if playing with her emotions was part of Jack's fun.

He'd toyed with her in life and seemed to continue with that tradition even now beyond the grave.

"What am I supposed to do now, Jack? Where do I go from here?" Rachel's heart was a broken record of disappointment and failure.

Chapter 17

Rain was due to head back to the States tomorrow and needed to go to the store to grab a few things. This trip had brought her many revelations—one being that the man she'd married was a total stranger to her. She was beyond ready to get back to the States and be in the company of her friends.

As she moved through the duplex, she sent out a group text and notified her friends that she'd be back late tomorrow evening and she'd fill them in over dinner. Prue was the first to respond.

Rain knew that Prue's life was a mess, too. She'd seen a segment on Prue on E News but hadn't reached out to check on her. Rain felt a pang of guilt as she realized she hadn't checked on her friend in quite some time.

She decided to take the time to send Prue a separate text message where she apologized for being a bad friend. Prue sent her back a winking emoji.

She grabbed a light jacket and told Patty she'd be back soon.

The store was only a few blocks away so Rain had decided to walk, despite the late hour. Patty told her to be careful and settled in the living room with a tub of cookie dough ice cream.

Rain closed the front door and locked it. Suddenly, someone grabbed her from behind and placed a hand over her mouth.

Rain instantly panicked and tried to scream, but the hand closed tighter over her mouth.

She instantly had flashbacks of being pinned under Derrick as he raped her against the window.

Her attacker tightened his hold on her and whispered in her ear. "You don't know how long I've been waiting to have you in my arms again."

Rain's eyes grew wide and she kicked back with a leg and hit the man. He grunted—she'd kicked his shin—and released her. Rain spun to find Derrick standing there. He massaged his shin and she swore.

"What are you doing here?" She fumbled with her keys and instantly tried to unlock the door. "Get out of here!" Rain began to beat on the door.

"C'mon, Rain! I just want to talk. I wasn't trying to scare you. I was trying to keep you from yelling. I never meant to hurt you. I'm messed up, okay?"

"Patty!" Rain shouted moments before the door swung open.

"Rain, what's—" Patty stopped as she caught sight of Derrick and her cousin's disheveled appearance. She pulled Rain into the house. "Call the police!" She tried to slam the door, but Derrick pushed against it.

Patty cried out and slammed the door, catching Derrick's hand in the door. He shouted and swore then began to beat against the door as Patty engaged the lock.

She turned and caught sight of Rain just standing there. "Call the police!" Patty shouted.

Rain ran off and Patty moved away from the door as Derrick continued to beat on it. Then he switched to kicking the door.

"He's trying to break in!" Patty shouted, rushing out of the room.

Patty rushed into the guest bedroom and found Rain. "I called the police. They're on the way!"

"Let's get upstairs!" Patty told her and they headed up the stairs just as Derrick kicked open the front door.

Rain shouted and they caught sight of Derrick as he moved into the house, pushing the door aside. He'd knocked it off its hinges.

"I just want to talk!" Derrick yelled.

Upstairs, Rain and Patty locked themselves into the bedroom and tried to barricade it.

"That's not going to stop him," Rain said.

"Where'd you meet this guy?" Patty asked.

Rain didn't have time to reply before a loud thud sounded. Derrick kicked at the door.

Patty pushed her cousin behind her. "Leave us alone!" she cried. She looked at Rain. "Try the window!"

"Rain, we're supposed to be together!" Derrick shouted as he began to kick at the door.

Rain tried to lift the window up, terror gripping her heart.

Patty caught sight of a baseball bat and reached for it seconds before Derrick kicked the door down.

Both women screamed as Derrick rushed into the room. Patty yelled and swung the bat, catching Derrick in the abdomen. He doubled over and Rain ran forward, slamming her fists into his back before she gripped the back of his head and drove her knee into his face.

She was nobody's victim. She was a woman!

Derrick yelled and blood gushed from his nose. He shoved Rain backwards as Patty came at him with the bat again. He ducked under the blow and tried to grab Patty.

"You broke my nose!" he yelled as blood fell onto his shirt.

Patty pulled her arms back and prepared to swing again, but Derrick was faster. He reached out and yanked the bat from her. Patty jumped backwards.

"Don't you touch her!" shouted Rain as she rushed across the room and shoved Derrick with all her might.

As he stumbled forward, Patty slid out her leg and tripped him. His momentum carried him forward and through the window.

"Derrick!!" screamed Rain as Patty gasped in shock.

Rain rushed to her cousin and helped her to her feet. They could hear sirens in the distance. Help was on the way.

The two women moved towards the shattered window and caught sight of Derrick lying unconscious on the lawn.

Patty grabbed Rain's hand and they rushed downstairs.

Two police cars pulled up just as Rain and Patty emerged outside.

"Freeze!" an officer yelled and both women raised their hands.

"Please, don't shoot!" cried Rain as the officer trained his gun on her.

Three other officers moved to the Caucasian officer's side.

"We live here!" said Patty. "He's over there!" She pointed and the four officers looked in the direction of where Patty pointed.

Three of the officers moved towards the side of the house and the sole female officer approached them. Rain moved after the three officers. She wanted to see Derrick's body. She wanted to see him lying in a pool of his blood on the grass.

He'd hurt her, he wasn't the man she'd married, and it was over.

As she rounded the corner, she found the officers standing among broken glass. They glanced around and one had his head angled upward to the broken window.

"Where is he?!" Rain shouted.

Behind her, Patty and the female officer rounded the corner and Rain heard Patty gasp.

Rain's mind went blank and she glanced from the broken window to the shards of glass and blood on the grass. Her face was twisted in horror.

"He's *gone*." And that was all Rain could mutter.

Chapter 18

❦ ❦ ❦ ❦ ❦ ❧ ❧ ❧ ❧ ❧

Miranda stood among the group of women she'd come to call her second family—the women that made up her Victims of Domestic Violence support group. She told the group that George was still "*missing*" and that she hoped he would stay gone for a few more months so she could file for divorce.

The courts required a statutory period of time to pass before they would grant her a divorce by default, along with full custody of her daughter, Piper. Miranda knew that George would never come back, but she continued the farce in public.

She brushed her hair back and continued to share. "I just know that my chains are broken…well, they will be. I still feel like sometimes George's ghost is still around, but I know that's just my guilt from staying with him so long. My only concern now is my child."

"Don't forget about your healing," said one of the ladies.

"This is my story now," Miranda said. "My chains are broken. I have to choose to be free and not let my past determine my future. My arms are wide open…I want to be happy. I used to ask

myself *'how did I get here?'* and *'where did I lose my way?'* But I
know that I was supposed to go through that period of struggle. I
was desperate to be set free…I'm not restless anymore. George can't
hurt me anymore."

"What if he comes back?" another women asked,
downtrodden.

Miranda eyed her. "These days I'm letting God handle all
things from above me. I can't worry about what goes on while I'm
on Earth. Life is too short. I have to live in the now."

George's ghost had only appeared to her a handful of times
and she'd since found a therapist to help her work through some of
her issues. She'd been a restless wife, but she refused to go forward
in that same manner. Now she just wanted to get Piper that same
help. Miranda knew that her daughter had suffered trauma at the
hands of her father and Miranda wanted to ensure that her child
wouldn't be weighed down by that pain forever.

"The sun will shine again," Miranda said as she took her
seat. "It'll shine in each of our lives. You just have to be desperate
for change."

"I want to be just like you when I grow up," said the woman
to Miranda's left.

Miranda smiled at her. "You're already the apple of my eye. I believe in you just like you believe in me." She looked around the room. "We're all in this together."

That evening, Miranda returned home and moved through the house. She looked at the closet she'd shared with George. She'd pulled some of his clothes off the hangers so it would appear like he'd left in a rush. Most of his clothes she'd simply donated to the local Salvation Army.

She'd figured everything out. Sure, she felt guilt or a moment of sadness would wash over her, but that was a small price to pay for the peace she'd brought to her and her daughter's lives.

Her life felt complete now. She was beginning to feel whole for the first time in years. Sure, she missed intimacy, but that was another sacrifice she was willing to give up. Sure, she craved companionship but with all the emotional scars on her heart and the physical scars on her body, Miranda wasn't sure if she'd ever find love again. Beyond that she wasn't even sure if she could trust another man.

Sometimes her heart ached like an open wound, but she'd live. She wouldn't die of a broken heart, that much she was sure of.

The doorbell rang and she was pulled from her thoughts. She opened the front door and found Rachel on her doorstep.

The two women embraced and Miranda welcomed her into the house. "I didn't catch you at a bad time, did I?"

Miranda shook her head. "You're fine." Miranda took in Rachel's entire being and smiled. "You're starting to look like yourself again."

Rachel playfully spun around to show off her entire outfit. "Do you like it?"

Miranda smiled. Rachel wore a yellow dress with strappy sandals and a matching headband. "Well, you look like *you*. I'm just glad that you're starting to get back to normal...you know, after..." She let the sentence trail off knowing Rachel would catch the drift.

"I'm just trying to find some sense of normalcy in this whole mess."

Miranda nodded. "It *has* been a little crazy for everyone lately, hasn't it?" Miranda recalled Rachel had told her and Freya about Jack's mistress and love child. She couldn't even imagine what Rachel was going through. She'd suffered so much in such a short span of time.

Rachel exhaled. "Yes, there's a lot going on for us all and it's not helping that Jack seems to be haunting me from his grave."

Miranda cringed at the comment. Her mind turned to George's unmarked grave deep in the woods.

"What are you going to do about the child?" Miranda asked, changing the subject.

"I saw the child. She looks just like Jack…but I'm not going to just give that slut money. She was a *cheerleader,* Miranda!"

"I've always been a nerd, Rachel. So, you know I automatically hate her regardless."

Rachel shook her head. "I still can't believe what she's told me. But I'm getting a blood test."

Miranda frowned. "I don't mean any harm, Rachel, but Jack's dead…How are you going to get a DNA test?"

Rachel looked at her friend and smiled coyly. "Jack has brothers…" Miranda was silent. When Rachel looked at her, she realized the woman was perplexed. "I've tried contacting them, but no one's returned my calls. I have one more brother to ask."

"Well that's smart, but how—"

"Gee, I thought you were a doctor?"

"I'm a botanist, not a geneticist!" exclaimed Miranda as Rachel pulled her phone from her purse.

Rachel rolled her eyes. "Well, a doctor is a doctor. There's a test called an avuncular test. It can be used to determine if a person is biologically related to a sibling of the father in question. Since Jack's deceased, it's pretty much the best option. Siblings share approximately 50% of their DNA, therefore an uncle shares about 25% of their DNA with the child in question. In this case, that would be Maria."

Rachel scrolled down her contact log and stopped on the name 'Jason Richards.'

"You're calling him now?"

Rachel shrugged. "He's the last brother."

Jason Richards walked through his loft in Savannah, Georgia. He was 6'2" with broad shoulders and possessed a swimmer's build. His abdominal area was defined and he currently showed it off as he stepped onto his balcony.

He wore slim fit jeans and was barefoot. Sunlight struck his skin and he groaned with pleasure at the warmth. His hair was brown and a little longer than ear-length.

He was sure of himself yet humble, unlike his older brother, Jack. Jason hadn't attended his funeral and hadn't reached out to his widow. However, as he relaxed on the balcony his thoughts turned to his sister-in-law.

He wondered how she was holding up. As far as he knew, Rachel and her brother hadn't had any kids so Jason was sure she was lonely.

He reached in his pocket and pulled his cellphone out. It was time to check on his sister-in-law.

Just as he was about to dial her number, his phone rang. He jumped and then grinned as Rachel's name appeared on his screen.

He accepted the call. "Well isn't this a coincidence! I was just about to call you!" His smooth tenor voice filled the air and he took a seat. Rachel's voice filled his ear and he grinned—flashing his dimples.

"Jason, I'm so glad you picked up!"

"I've been meaning to check on you. I really was about to call you. It's crazy how you called. You must've been thinking about me, too?"

Rachel laughed nervously and Jason realized he probably shouldn't flirt with his dead brother's wife.

"I need your help," she told him, pulling him from his thoughts.

"Anything, Red," he replied. "What's up?"

Back on Lyfe Road, Rachel grinned to herself and tucked a strand of red hair behind her ear.

Minutes later, Rachel ended the call. She ran a hand through her growing tresses and then smiled at Miranda.

"Sometimes you shock me," Miranda told her, staring at her in awe.

Rachel chuckled. "I'm going to make *sure* that slut doesn't see the light of day if that child isn't Jack's! Jason's going to fly up to the clinic to help with the DNA test." She grabbed her purse and turned to Miranda. "Well, let's go, girlfriend."

Miranda's eyes grew wide. "Wh-What? *Me?*"

Rachel placed a hand on her hip. "Yes, **you**. Do you see any of my other best friends here? Rain's in Liverpool, Freya's going through as the old woman who lived in a shoe, and Prue's getting settled at my house. So, sweetie, you're the only one left."

Miranda blew raspberries. "That makes me feel soooo much better knowing I'm your last resort," she sarcastically replied.

Rachel threw her arm over Miranda's shoulder, kissed her cheek, and led her friend to the front door.

Chapter 19

❧ ❧ ❧ ❧ ❧ ❧ ❧ ❧ ❧ ❧ ❧

Thursday, April 19, 2007

Prue had finally settled into Rachel's guest room. She plopped down on the bed and grabbed her cellphone. She had a missed call from her mother and another from her attorney. She checked her messages and realized that her attorney had left a voicemail. She clicked the message and listened. Her attorney was just calling to inform her that he'd received documents from Donatello's attorney. The divorce proceedings would begin soon.

She exhaled and then checked her text messages. There were several messages, but the only one that caught her eye was the text from Romeo.

I miss you, Prue. Please understand, I never meant to hurt you. I just didn't know how you would react if I told you. Please, let's have dinner and talk through this. I need you.

Prue sighed and wondered what she should do. He'd already given her HIV…what else did she have to lose?

After having time to process things, Prue realized she needed closure before she could move on. So, she decided to text Romeo back.

Sometimes I miss you, too, but I don't know if I can forgive you. Let's meet at that French restaurant we went to that time and we can talk then. -P

She'd been vague on purpose. If Romeo wanted her as much as he said then he should be acclimated to her favorite restaurants and activities, and other personal things.

She just wanted closure. That was all she wanted from him.

That evening, she arrived at 'Abel'—a small French restaurant downtown—and was surprised to see that Romeo was already there. Warmth filled her heart and Prue blushed.

Perhaps Romeo knew her better than she'd thought. Perhaps they could carve out their own path and then she shook her head. Things had changed.

He'd infected her with HIV. Why was she contemplating a future with him?

She moved across the upscale restaurant dressed in a simple Dior dress and heels. Her dark hair hung down her back.

Romeo caught sight of her and rose to his feet. "Hello, Prue."

"Hi," she said, trying to take the anger out of her voice.

He reached to hug her but she didn't allow it—pretending she hadn't seen him open his arms. Romeo flushed with embarrassment and took his seat.

"It's so good to see you."

Prue didn't look at him—she couldn't. Instead, she picked up the wine menu. She pretended to look it over for a moment before she placed it aside and looked at Romeo.

"I don't want to pretend that I'm okay, Romeo. My life is in shambles right now. I acknowledge that I played a part in all of this, but I need you to acknowledge your part, too."

He placed his menu aside. "I'm sorry for what I did, Prue. It wasn't right and I apologize. But in all honesty, I love you. It was wrong for me to not disclose my status and—"

"It was wrong for you not to tell me you were bisexual, either. I'm not homophobic, but it should've been my choice if I wanted to get into a situation with someone who went both ways. However, that's an entirely different conversation."

"It really bothers you that I dated Kelsey, doesn't it?"

Prue's stomach knotted and she balled her fist. She shook her head and tucked a strand of hair behind her ear. "That's a separate issue. Let's focus on what's truly important: *me*. It should've been my choice and I think that's why I'm more hurt than anything. You should've had enough decency enough to *tell me* and then allow me to decide if I wanted to take things to the next level. The fact that you took my choice in the matter away really bothers me. I should've been the one to decide whether or not I wanted to have unprotected sex with someone that has HIV."

He reached across the table and placed his hand atop hers. Prue forced herself not to pull away.

"Prue, I was *wrong.* I don't want to lose you. I regret making that decision for you. But let me just say this: I love you, Prudence. If I have to apologize every day for the rest of my life I will, but I cannot lose you."

She slowly pulled her hand away as the waiter walked up to the table to take their drink orders. Prue ordered a glass of White Zinfandel and waited until the waiter left the table before she spoke. "Tell me what happened."

Romeo rose an eyebrow. "You want to know how it happened?"

She swallowed. "I want to know everything…I *need* to know. If…*if* we're going to find a way back to each other then we can't have any secrets between us."

Both his eyebrows rose in surprise. "You're giving me another chance?"

She raised a hand. "Slow down, tiger. We will see...I can't ignore our history...We've been through a lot together and—"

"I love you," he told her. "You can't forget that. I can't imagine not being with you. I can't imagine another man with his hands around you. I want you...I always have."

"I just hate this part...the indecision." Prue sighed. "I want to..." She didn't know what she wanted. The world was crashing all around her. Was this the part where the end of the road began? She didn't want to be alone...She didn't know how.

But did she want to be with the man who'd inflicted an incurable disease on her?

It seemed that she and Romeo were bound by the laws of the same routine. He'd hurt her, she'd left, and then had come back. It had been the same thing with Donatello.

She didn't want to begin a relationship that was doomed to fail from the start. But she already knew she and Romeo wouldn't last...

The disease would claim one of them sooner than later and Prue felt it would claim her first if she couldn't get on antiretroviral drugs soon.

She took a deep breath. "No more lies, Romeo. I want to know everything. How long have you been bisexual? Were you fooling around with men while we were together? I need to know everything…"

And another one bites the dust, Prue thought as he began to finally reveal his truth. She was falling back into the broken record of Romeo and Prue. *Why can I not conquer love?* She asked herself.

She felt numb as he told her about the first time he realized he was into guys. He'd been 16 and had just embarked on his modeling career. He'd broken things off with his first serious girlfriend only a week before he'd been flown to Paris for a photoshoot.

The photographer there had—

"You know what," said Prue, interrupting him. "Let's just get out of here."

Romeo was confused. She rose from the table. She felt numb and just wanted to feel alive.

She was sick and tired of being sick and tired. If she and Romeo were going to be together, she needed to feel alive again. He'd brought her to life at one point…and she needed to feel that way again.

She knew that their 'love'—if it could be called that—would never last, but she didn't want to be alone. She'd rather have somebody than nobody.

"What's wrong?" Romeo asked.

You're just like poison, she thought as she took him in. *You gave me this disease and it's slowly moving through my system and breaking all of my defenses with time.*

"You used to make love to me," she said. Romeo looked around the restaurant making sure no one had heard her.

"Lower your voice, Prue," he told her as he pulled his wallet out and placed several bills on the table.

"I don't want you to make love to me, Romeo. I need you to fuck me. I need you to—"

Romeo moved over to her and shushed her. He grabbed her hand. "You don't have to tell me twice." He led her out of the restaurant as the waiter arrived at the table with her glass of wine and his Vodka tonic.

Prue felt like her soul had left her body and she was watching herself from a different point of view. Romeo led her out to his car. He helped her into his rental car and they headed to his hotel.

Regrets collected like old friends and Prue could feel her regrets piling up. She'd been a fool once and she'd been blind. She couldn't leave the past behind because it was destroying her present and killing her chances at a future. Her past mistakes clung to her like sweaty clothes.

But this evening, she was going to bury her fears and insecurities and find some semblance of normalcy.

Romeo led her into his hotel room and began to kiss her. She forced her issues out of her mind.

Back when she was Happy-Prue she used to like to throw her hands up in the air. Back then she'd thought she could count on Romeo. But now she was Numb-Prue. Trying to process every emotion was just too much, and things went wrong no matter what she did.

Her life was just too rough. Romeo raised her hands and placed them on his shoulders. He kissed her tenderly and then unzipped her dress.

Prue slid out of it and wondered if Happy-Prue would ever return. Romeo told her he loved her…but she didn't believe him.

Sooner or later in life the things you love, you lose…and Prue felt she was going to lose her health and thus nothing else mattered to her. She was going to lose *everything*.

So why not be reckless? She thought to herself.

She just wanted to *feel* **right now**! She *needed* to feel.

Romeo caressed her soft skin.

I'm going to die, she thought as Romeo unhooked her bra. She tilted her head back and looked at the ceiling. She wondered if God was watching right now.

Lord, I just don't care…

"I love you so much," Romeo whispered in her ear as she helped him undress.

She moved towards the queen size bed and removed her panties. Romeo was erect when he turned to move towards the bed.

Prue exhaled and tried to focus on her own body. She was mindful that her pulse was steady. Her breathing was even. But what was the use of being conscious of her body? She felt that her life was over and now she just waited for death to claim her.

She didn't want to be alone tonight, or ever. She would get what intimacy she could. She would take love where she could find it.

Romeo wanted her and she knew that by having HIV no other man would…unless he, too, was positive.

She needed Romeo to light her fire and take control. Her life was no longer her own—he'd taken it from her. So why control every aspect of it from now on?

She wrapped her arms around him and he buried his face in her neck as he tasted her and breathed her in. Prue closed her eyes and exhaled.

His body was hard—rock hard abs and a solid build—yet comfortable against Prue's. He wanted her and she could tell. And then Prue recalled a time when she'd wanted him, too.

She forced herself to pull *that* version of herself to the forefront. And when ***that*** Prue emerged she was just fine.

Prue wrapped her legs over his hips and crossed them—pulling him closer. The way he touched her and kissed her helped to minimize the numbness.

Slowly but surely, she felt her heart and soul thaw.

"*Romeo.*" And that was all she needed to say. He looked into her eyes and kissed her tenderly.

He slid into her—unprotected—and she closed her eyes again.

Dread chilled her stomach. She recalled a conversation with her doctor where the doctor had informed her of the risk of having unprotected sex when both partners were HIV positive.

The doctor had informed her that unprotected sex when both partners were HIV positive was still risky because of the potential for an HIV superinfection. Superinfection occurred when a person who was already HIV positive was exposed to and became infected with a different strain of the virus.

But Prue wondered if she should be worried about that. Romeo was the one who'd infected her. They had the same strain of HIV, right?

Then Prue recalled that superinfection was problematic because it was harder to treat, even when using combined antiretroviral medicine as there was a possibility that someone could be infected with two different drug-resistant strains.

"I love you," Romeo groaned, kissing her. Prue was pulled from her thoughts and opened her eyes, kissing him back.

She'd forgotten that they were having sex. She'd been so deep inside her own mind that the outside world had passed her by.

"Forgive me, Prue. I need you. I don't know what I'd do if I lost you."

"You won't have to find out," she replied in a voice just above a whisper. "I'm not going anywhere."

She wrapped her arms around him and kissed him moments before he pulled out of her and began to kiss a trail down her midsection.

Fear lingered beneath the surface, but Prue was more fearful of losing him to the world than living with their combined demons.

The bond between them was fragile but Romeo was determined to mend that wound.

Romeo settled between her legs and held her open as he sucked on her clit. Prue moaned and arched her back, bringing him closer to her sex.

She felt the pressure build up as he took her into his mouth and sucked hard and then flicked his warm, wet tongue over her.

Prue grabbed a fistful of his hair with one hand and grabbed the bedsheet with the other. Her legs began to tremble and she knew she was about to climax.

Prue cried out as she came. Romeo moved to slide into her again and smiled down at her—his face covered in her essence.

Romeo then sank into her, possessing her body with every inch. When all of him was within her, he began to move his hips.

Prue clutched him to her moments before he took her left nipple into his mouth. "*Romeo!*" she cried out, losing herself as he hammered into her.

He gripped her face and they locked eyes as he continued to move inside of her. "Look at me, Prue. Don't be afraid. Make love *to* me. Be here *with* me."

Prue struggled to get past the apprehension, the fear, and the anger. She simply kissed him and then moved her mouth to his ear. *"Fuck love, just fuck **me**."*

He groaned from deep within his chest as he came within her and in that moment, Prue felt a tear leave her eye and she quickly wiped it away.

Romeo slid out of her and rolled to the other side of the bed and exhaled as he wiped sweat from his brow.

Prue silently slid out of bed and headed to the bathroom, locking the door behind her.

She refused to look at herself in the mirror. She climbed into the shower and cried.

Chapter 20

❧❧❧❧❧❧❧❧❧❧❧

May 5, 2007

Rachel Richards was anxious beyond measure. Today was the day the DNA test would be conducted. Her brother-in-law, Jason Richards, stood at her side as they waited for Robin and Maria to arrive.

Rachel glanced at Jason and saw that his face was relaxed. She was surprised at how handsome he was. She hadn't recalled him being so good looking, but then again, she hadn't seen him since her wedding. Back then, Jason had been a lanky teen.

"You ready for this?" he asked when he caught her staring.

She composed herself and nodded. "As ready as I'll ever be."

He nodded and turned away from her to glance out the window. Rachel followed his gaze and caught sight of Robin and Maria walking towards the entrance.

Rachel smoothed her hands over her skirt and moved to meet Robin at the door. "Oh, Robin, dear, I'm so glad you're on time."

"Well, aren't you in a chipper mood," Robin replied as she eyed the man just behind Rachel. Perhaps he was her bodyguard.

Rachel knelt and spoke to the child. Robin nodded towards the man. "Who's the hunk?"

Rachel rose to her feet and smiled sweetly. "He's another man you *can't* fuck."

Robin bristled at the remark.

Jason stepped forward and extended his hand. "I'm Jason, Jack's brother."

Rachel knocked his hand away before Robin could touch him. "He's here to help with the DNA test."

Robin's eyes grew wide. "H-How can he help? He's not Maria's father!"

"You're right, he's not," said Rachel, grinning. "But he and Jack *were* brothers. They share DNA and if your little girl is Jack's then she should share DNA with Jason."

Robin shook her head. "I don't think that will work." She looked at her daughter.

"What's wrong?" Jason asked, teasing her. "Having a change of heart?"

Robin ignored him and just looked at Rachel. "Why can't you just stick to what Jack had in place? There was a plan."

"She's not stupid like my brother," Jason said.

Robin clenched her jaw. "Let's do this then."

Rachel grinned and led the woman to the counter to sign in. "Uh, Rachel, can I talk to you for a minute?" asked Jason.

"Sure." She looked at Robin. "Excuse me for a minute. Go ahead and sign in, though."

Jason pulled Rachel into a corner and turned his back to Robin. "That little girl doesn't look *anything* like Jack. I don't think she's his."

Rachel frowned and looked over his shoulder and at the little girl. The child played with a doll. Rachel sucked in a breath. "Her eyes, Jason…they remind me of Jack. And it's like when I look at her, I can almost picture Jack staring back at me."

"But—"

She looked at him. "I just want to make sure… Please, just do this for me."

Jason exhaled sharply and nodded. "Alright, Rachel."

He turned to leave but Rachel touched his bicep and he stopped. She was surprised by how firm it was. She withdrew her hand. "I promise you, if that little girl isn't Jack's then Robin is going to pay for the hell she's put me through."

Jason's brow creased. "I hope you aren't planning anything crazy."

Rachel grinned menacingly. "I'm not going to kill her…I'm just going to ruin her."

Jason laughed and walked off.

Three hours had past and the three adults continued to wait for the rapid test results. Rachel returned to the waiting room after making a phone call.

Rachel looked across the waiting room and caught sight of Maria. The child was asleep, her head in her mother's lap. Robin rocked nervously.

Rachel felt a twinge of disappointment at being unable to bare a child. She wanted a child so badly.

I don't know what I'll do if she turns out to be Jack's daughter. God, it's going to hurt so bad.

Rachel felt a lump rising in her throat and she couldn't shake the nervous feeling in her stomach. She jumped when Jason tapped her arm.

"Are you okay? You look like you're barely holding it together."

Rachel rose to her feet and rushed to the restroom. Robin watched as she left and suddenly looked worried.

Robin rose from her seat and pulled her sleeping child into her arms.

"Where are you going?" Jason asked as the woman moved towards the exit.

Robin turned and looked at Jason, tears brimming her eyes. "I-I can't do this anymore. I feel awful."

"Why?" Jason asked.

"I—"

Rachel exited the restroom and made a beeline to them, but Jason caught sight of her and gestured for her to stay back. She nodded and hung back.

"What's going on?" he asked Robin.

"Rachel's a good person. I-I can't keep doing this."

"Can't keep doing what?" he asked her, his pulse quickening.

"Yes, I slept with Jack, but…but—"

"But what?" Jason asked, stepping closer to her.

Robin sucked in a breath and shook her head. "He isn't Maria's father. I just…I convinced him that he was."

"So why lie on my brother?! Why make all of this up?"

Rachel quickly moved over to them as Jason's volume increased and eyes turned to watch. The receptionist rose to her feet.

"Jason?"

"It's all a lie, Rachel," Jason told her. He glared at Robin. "Why would you lie?"

Rachel looked at her. "Is it true?"

"Jack provided for us ever since I told him I was pregnant."

You were such an idiot, Jack! Rachel thought. "She isn't his?" she asked, confirming it.

Robin shook her head and a tear fell. "I'm so, so sorry. I just didn't know how we'd make it if Jack wasn't paying the bills. I was restless and desperate."

"How dare you?!" shouted Jason.

"Sir!" called the receptionist. "Please lower your voice."

Rachel took a step back and felt like she could breathe again. Jack hadn't fathered a child outside of their marriage…at least this time. There might be other bastards out there, but at least for now it was over.

I'm sorry, Jack, she thought as she ran a hand over her face. Rachel looked at Robin. "May God have mercy on your soul because no one else will."

Robin clutched her daughter to her chest and ran out of the clinic.

"Rachel, I'm sorry," Jason said.

"Don't be," she told him, her eyes locked on Robin as she attempted to leave the clinic. "It's not over." She pulled him along as she moved towards the exit.

Jason gasped as he took in the sight.

Outside, Robin had run into a frenzy of flashing lights. Rachel had stepped out to make a few phone calls after the DNA test. She had contacted all the major media outlets she could with the help of Miranda. They'd reported that Robin had been trying to extort money from her in a quest to destroy Jack's name and fabricate a story that Jack had fathered her child.

Rachel hadn't been sure of what the DNA results would be when she'd placed the calls, but either way she wanted to get Robin back for what she'd done. Luckily things had turned out in Rachel's favor.

And the media responded by flooding the clinic's parking lot with paparazzi and reporters. Photographers snapped shots of the shameless woman and her child as reporters shouted questions.

Rachel and Jason watched from inside the clinic as Robin Martez was harassed.

"They're going to break her like she broke me," Rachel confessed.

Jason wrapped his arm around her shoulder. "You're going to be alright. I can tell I won't have to worry about you." Rachel grinned up at him.

Jason couldn't believe how the photographers were harassing Robin—crowding around her and yelling. Jason could hear the child's cries above the uproar.

"You always knew that she wasn't his, didn't you?"

Rachel didn't reply right away. Instead, she continued to watch Robin. "There was always something deep down that doubted her, but to be honest…I knew my husband." She turned in Jason's embrace. "It was a possibility."

Jason exhaled and moved his arm off Rachel's shoulder. "Yeah, my brother was a piece of work, wasn't he?"

Rachel absentmindedly pulled her brother-in-law's arm back over her shoulder. "Now I can move on. Now I can breathe again. It's time for me to start over."

Jason looked at her and they walked out of the clinic, avoiding the crowd. "What are you going to do?"

Rachel smiled. "I'm going to live my life."

She shrugged his arm off and moved into the sunlight. She stretched her arms out to her side and tilted her face towards the noonday sun.

"*Hello, world!* Did you miss me?" she yelled as a weight lifted itself off her shoulders.

Rachel Adams Richards was ready to live *her* life on her own terms for the first time in nearly thirteen years!

Jason laughed as he watched her.

Rachel spun and soaked up warmth from the sun. Now, she could begin again.

*So, **this** is what freedom feels like?* She thought to herself.

Her life was once again her own.

May 15, 2007

Miranda Jordan-Copeland flipped through the daily newspaper and landed on the ad she'd placed announcing her intent to divorce George. Even though she knew it was all for show, she had to keep up the farce.

She'd been running the ad daily for over eight weeks.

She needed to prove to the courts that she'd been actively "looking" for George. She was ready to be legally untied to George.

She tossed the newspaper aside and glanced at the clock. Piper would be home from school soon.

"We need a change," Miranda told herself as she rose from the couch and headed outdoors to wait for her daughter in front of the house.

Just as Miranda exited through the front door, Piper's bus pulled up and deposited Piper and the five Goodchild children onto Lyfe Road.

Miranda waved at Francesca and the others as they ran down the street and headed to Freya's house. Piper ran up the driveway calling for her mother.

Miranda's heart swelled with love at the sight of her daughter. "I'm so glad you're home!"

Piper hugged her mother and Miranda squeezed her tight. "How was your day, honey?"

"It was good, Mommy."

"I'm glad to hear that." Miranda knelt before her daughter. "What do you think about us taking a little vacation?"

Piper's eyes grew wide. "Wow! That would be fun." She began to jump up and down. "Let's go to the beach! No, no, Disney World!"

Miranda grinned. "How about we go visit Auntie Rain and then go to Disney World?"

Piper shrugged. "I guess that's okay."

Miranda laughed and led Piper back into the house. Yes, she needed a break from the white Colonial dwelling with black shutters that she called home.

Miranda quickly went about planning a trip to the UK, but first she'd have to call and ask Rain. They hadn't talked much since she'd left.

She wasn't supposed to have been gone so long, but undoubtedly Rain was going to make Liverpool her permanent home. Whatever had happened between her and Derrick had changed everything.

Miranda worried about her friend, but all she could do was reach out. Rain had to want help and if she didn't want to talk about it, Miranda couldn't and *wouldn't* make her.

Perhaps she just needed space. But it had been over two months. How much time did someone need before they talked to their friends?

When Rain didn't answer the phone, Miranda left a voicemail for her friend to call her back and then she pulled out her laptop. Disney World at this time of year would be absolutely incredible!

It was time for Miranda to put her daughter first.

Piper's birthday was coming up and she'd be seven. Her memories would last a lifetime and it was time for Miranda to help Piper make happy ones.

Miranda was finally feeling the sensation people called *freedom.*

*** June 2, 2007***

Freya Goodchild caressed her growing belly as she sat on the examination table at her OBGYN's office.

"You're about fourteen weeks," her doctor said. "Your twins are healthy. You're healthy. Everything is fine."

Freya grinned and the doctor wiped the gel off her belly. Freya pulled her blouse down and wondered if now was a good time to let her new boss know she was pregnant.

She'd only recently returned to the working world and this pregnancy was happening at the worst possible time. She pulled out her blackberry and sent an e-mail to her boss requesting a meeting at his earliest convenience.

She was beginning to show, but thankfully billowy blouses had hidden her growing belly. Freya thanked her OBGYN and headed out of the office.

She glanced at her phone and realized she was going to be late. Ever since she'd caught Aaron cheating on her she'd been seeing a therapist.

There were so many things going on in her life. She was carrying twins, juggling five kids, and still adjusting to her new job. Not to mention that she and Aaron were still in the preliminary stages of divorce.

As Freya drove across town for her appointment, she thanked God for the strength that she still possessed. Life was stressful, but it wasn't overwhelming anymore. And for that, she was thankful.

Though she was anxious about the future and what it would hold for her and her children, she tried to keep her focus on the present. Her journey to freedom was ongoing.

*** June 3, 2007 ***

Prue knocked on Rachel's door and waited for her to say 'come in.' She was nervous. She'd been living with Rachel for a few weeks and things had been relatively smooth. She hadn't booked a gig since she'd left the hospital and hadn't heard from Romeo in a few days.

But today she was going to come clean. She needed to tell someone besides her mother. No one else knew she was HIV positive, and it was eating away at her.

She needed someone to talk to.

"Come in," said Rachel. Prue opened the door and found Rachel in bed with the newspaper—her curtains drawn.

"Morning, Rae. Are you busy?" Prue asked, still dressed in pajamas.

Rachel placed the newspaper aside. "Not at all, come on in. I was just reading Miranda's article. You know they still haven't found George."

Prue cringed at the mention of the man that had abused her best friend for years. She climbed into bed beside Rachel.

"I need to tell you something," Prue said, rubbing her palms together. She was beyond nervous.

"What is it?" Rachel said, her smile fading. Prue exhaled sharply and placed a hand over her face.

Rachel gripped her friend's hand. "What's so bad that you're about to have a breakdown? Are you back with Romeo?"

Prue dropped her hand and looked at Rachel. "How'd you know?"

Rachel shrugged. "I saw him drop you off the other day."

"You didn't say anything."

Rachel cocked her head. "It wasn't my place to bring it up. I figured you'd share when you were ready."

"Does it bother you?"

Rachel patted Prue's hand. "Sweetie, it's not my place to judge. As long as you're happy that's all that matters…You're happy, aren't you?"

Prue shrugged. "Sometimes." She exhaled; this was it. "Rachel, I have HIV."

Rachel was shocked into silence. She opened her mouth to speak and then thought better of it. She cleared her throat and grabbed Prue's hand with both of hers. "Are you okay?" Prue shook her head and began to cry. Rachel pulled her friend into her arms. "It's going to be alright, Prue. How long have you known? Have you told—"

"I've only told my mom and Donatello. You're the first of the girls to know." She pulled away and wiped her eyes. "I wanted to tell you sooner, but Jack had just died when I found out and I just…I didn't want to burden you."

Rachel climbed out of bed and went to fetch her some tissue. "Oh, honey, you didn't have to worry about me. I would've been able to be there for you and grieve at the same time."

"I know, but still…"

"Have you started a regimen? There's this guy I knew in college that was on pills that helped…"

"I just started taking antiretrovirals a few weeks ago…"

Rachel nodded. "So, you told Donatello? How'd that go?"

"About as well as expected," Prue replied.

"That would mean that Romeo…" Rachel trailed off as she realized what that meant. "Oh, *Prue.*"

Prue shook her head. "Don't judge me, Rachel. I can't handle it right now."

"Did Romeo know before he gave it to you?"

"Does it matter?" Prue asked, going on the defensive. Rachel held up her hands in mock surrender. "All that matters is that I have it, we're still together, and Donatello is furious."

"I bet he is," Rachel said under her breath. "I'm going to pour a glass of wine. Would you like some?"

"Rae, it's barely nine in the morning."

Rachel shrugged. "It's happy hour somewhere." She climbed back out of bed and headed to the kitchen. Prue followed her. "So, are you okay, Prue… really?"

"Not in the slightest," she responded as she slid onto a bar stool. Rachel reached into a cabinet and pulled out a pair of wine glasses and then found a bottle of Merlot.

"You've been going through this all by yourself for months. I don't know how you're still standing."

"I'm barely managing to stay upright."

"You didn't have to go through this alone. The day the girls and I visited you in the hospital—"

"I would've told you all then, but Romeo showed up."

Rachel's head bobbed, recalling that he'd showed up less than five minutes into their visit.

"Prue, I love you. Your friends love you. I'm in your corner."

"I guess I just didn't want to include everyone in my drama…I've felt so dirty and now nothing I do will get me clean."

Rachel handed Prue a glass of wine and quickly took a sip before she spoke. "Prue, we're all going through something… Each and every one of us has something going wrong in our lives. But the beauty of living is that things get better. We need each other. You can't be afraid of needing your friends."

Rachel moved across the kitchen and took a seat next to her friend. "I hate being restless just as much as the next person, but restlessness is a part of life. It's God's way of letting us know that we need to work a little harder to find peace."

Prue sighed. "I just don't know what to do or where to go from here...I've been feeling so numb and vulnerable."

"And you think staying with Romeo is going to fix that?"

Prue looked at her. "That's just it, *I don't know.*"

Rachel placed her glass on the counter and took both of Prue's hands into hers. "We won't be restless forever. Hell, we weren't even *wives* forever." She chuckled, causing Prue to chuckle, too. "This continuous cycle of hurt, loss, and struggle won't last forever. We'll make it through these storms together. We just have to trust the process."

"Trust the process?" asked Prue.

Rachel nodded. "We're all on our own individual journeys to freedom. You just have to find a path that will help you find your own sense of freedom...You have to get back out into the world, Prue." She cocked her head. "You've been hiding, haven't you?"

When Prue didn't answer, Rachel had her answer.

"Listen to me, Prudence, you're still young. You're still healthy. Live your life while you can. Call your manager or whoever you need to and get back to work. Modeling made you happy."

"But—"

"No, honey. You need to live your life."

"But what if someone finds out…?"

Rachel frowned. "You never cared what people thought of you before. When I first met you, you came to your door in lingerie with your little goodies on display for the entire street. Where's that bold woman I met all those years ago?"

"I have no idea…" Prue took another sip from her glass. "I wish I knew where she was."

Rachel placed a finger in the center of Prue's chest. "She's in there, Prue. You just have to tap into her. There's still time left in your hourglass to get it together. You can do this."

"You think so?"

Rachel waved her friend's words off. "I have no doubt that you can do this. You'll be fine, Prudence. Just because you've been diagnosed with this disease doesn't mean you stop living. We're all still fighting for peace. Don't you throw in the towel now. Make HIV your bitch."

Prue laughed at hearing Rachel curse.

Rachel smiled and raised her glass. "To freedom."

Prue smiled sweetly and raised her glass. "To freedom."

The two women clinked their glasses and raised their glasses to their lips as they drank.

*** June 5, 2007***

After Derrick had attacked Patty and Rain, Rain had cancelled her flight and prolonged her trip. The authorities were sure that Derrick had gone back to the States but hadn't been able extradite him. So, until they could have Derrick brought up on charges, Rain decided to stay put.

Patty was happy to have her and Rain was thankful. She'd been back in Liverpool for months and had no intentions on returning to America any time soon. Her life there was over.

The doorbell rang and Rain moved downstairs to answer the door. She was hoping it was the mailman with her package. She'd been waiting on a delivery for weeks.

Rain peeked through the peephole and caught sight of a stack of boxes. Someone stood on the porch with two boxes in their hands, but Rain couldn't tell if it was male or female.

She opened the door.

"Special delivery," said the person on the doorstep and Rain realized it was a man.

She instantly recognized the voice and moved backwards, trying to close the door. The man moved the boxes to the side and Rain looked upon the face of her husband—a man she hadn't seen since he'd attacked her and Patty.

"Derrick, you need to leave. Right now," she said, her voice strong and devoid of emotion. *Fake it until you make it,* she thought to herself.

"I just wanted to bring some of your things to you," he told her, grinning but his eyes were blank. She didn't see a soul inside when she gazed at him.

"You could've just mailed them. Now please leave."

Derrick dropped the boxes and yanked her outside. Rain yelled and Derrick shook her—shaking her into silence.

"Will you stop it already?!" he shouted. "I'm not going to hurt you."

"We both know that's not true. Are you on drugs or something? What's wrong with you?" She'd grown afraid of her husband. His behavior had turned erratic and he'd changed before her eyes.

"There was so much going on back then, Rain. I'm not the same man I was, I promise. I'm not a monster. I was just…hurting."

"Whether or not you were hurting, that doesn't excuse your behavior! You could've killed me and Patty. You nearly killed *me*!"

"I'm sorry, Rain. I wasn't myself. But I don't know why I even try because you don't want me anymore. I would rather leave before I hurt you…but I can't walk away. I love you, Rain. Please just come home."

"No," she told him. "It's over, Derrick. You need to get some help."

"You hate me, don't you? I see it in your eyes. Look, Rain, my home doesn't feel like a home anymore. I need you. What can I do to get you to come back?"

"There's nothing you can say or do. The damage is done. Please, just go. You're embarrassing yourself."

"If I knew better, I would do—"

"See, the thing is I *know* your mama raised you better. Something changed, Derrick. It's like one day you woke up and were missing screws."

"Donatello…he—"

"What does he have to do with who you've become?" she asked, growing frustrated.

"Everything."

"All I want you to do is go away."

"It's like I can't get out of my own way. I hope that God will forgive you for leaving me. Marriage is supposed to be sacred."

"And you were supposed to love me, not hurt me." Rain turned to go back into the house, but he grabbed her by the wrist and pulled her close. He kissed her and held onto her tightly.

Rain slapped him and tried to pull away. "You're delusional, Derrick! Let me go!"

"Don't try to fight it. I know you still love me, girl."

She slapped him and then kneed him in the gonads. Derrick released her and she tried to open the door but it had locked behind her.

She moved towards the steps and tried to run off the porch, but Derrick grabbed her again.

"Don't touch me!" she shouted before she spat in his face.

Derrick growled in frustration as Rain ran off the porch and headed towards the street.

"Help!!" she screamed as she ran out of the front yard. "Somebody help me!"

"Rain!" Derrick shouted from behind her as he gave chase.

"HELP!" she shouted as she ran along the sidewalk.

"Rain, stop!" Derrick shouted as he sped up, trying to catch up to her.

Rain looked over her shoulder. Her heart raced and adrenaline filled her. She knew if Derrick caught up to her it was all over. He wasn't going to leave her alone.

Their love affair had turned into a nightmare. As she ran down the street flashes of the rape and the attack at the duplex filled her mind. Terror filled her and she wished she could pinpoint when Derrick had changed on her.

Things had gone from good to worse in such a short time. If she'd known then what she had come to learn now she would've never given him her number when they'd first met.

She ran harder. Her lungs burned and she realized he was catching up. "No!" she cried, pushing herself harder. "Somebody help me! Please!"

"RAIN!!!" he shouted.

Her muscles screamed for her to slow down, to stop. But Rain knew if she stopped it would be over.

Derrick would catch up to her and he'd hurt her.

All she craved now was freedom.

Rain turned and ran into the street.

She closed her eyes. *Forgive me.*

"Rain!!" Derrick screamed as a horn blared.

He skidded to a stop and watched in horror as Rain was struck and then run over by a double decker bus.

To be continued in

PART III...

Author's Note:

I initially wrote 'The Wives 2' from November 16, 2008-May 28, 2009. However, during the editing phase in December 2018-January 2019, I found myself changing so much of the original story. *inserts winking emoji*

While editing the story I listened to music. Music gets my creative juices flowing and truly inspires me during my writing process.

As you re-read the novel, listen to the playlist/soundtrack to get a better feeling of the 'vibe' of this story. Music definitely motivated scenes throughout the story.

Without further ado, here's a list of songs I listened to on repeat while *'Journey to Freedom'* was compiled.

Journey to Freedom Soundtrack

1. Chapter 1- Imagine | Ariana Grande

2. Chapter 2- Heaven | Beyoncé

3. Chapter 3- The Races | The Bird & the Bee

4. Chapter 4- Breathin' | Ariana Grande

5. Chapter 5- Baby | The Bird & the Bee

6. Chapter 6- One More Chance | Jackson 5

7. Chapter 7- Pray You Catch Me | Beyoncé

8. Chapter 8- From Time | Drake ft Jhené Aiko

9. Chapter 9- Summertime Sadness | Lana Del Rey

10. Chapter 10- Pyschobabble | FrouFrou

11. Chapter 11- Flicks | FrouFrou

12. Chapter 12- Commitment | Monica

13. Chapter 13- Pink + White | Frank Ocean

14. Chapter 14- Pyramids | Frank Ocean

15. Chapter 15- 2 | H.E.R.

16. Chapter 16- Un-Break My Heart | Toni Braxton

17. Chapter 17- I'm Upset | Drake

18. Chapter 18- Jungle | Drake

19. Chapter 19- Pretty Wicked Things | Dawn Richard

20. Chapter 20- 86 | Dawn Richard

   - Dancing With a Stranger | Sam Smith ft. Normani

*** _About the Author_ ***

Jay, as a child, discovered that his life could be a whirlwind of adventures by simply opening a book and reading. To this day, reading is still his favorite thing in the world, followed closely by watching movies. He still has a fondness for fantasy, sci-fi, and fiction, which is probably why he writes for those genres.

When Jay DeMoir isn't working on his next book, he's usually binge-watching old TV shows on DVD or making music or teaching young minds.

Jay DeMoir is not only an alumnus of the University of Memphis, where he received his BA in Communications (Film& Video Production) and minored in English Literature and Psychology, but also an educator. During the day, he's a Middle School English/Language Arts teacher and currently seeking his master's degree in education.

Another hat he wears is that of CEO of a multimedia company 'House of DeMoir Productions.' Jay DeMoir is also a filmmaker, registered screenwriter, and musician that has seen his stories brought to life as web shows, documentaries, and musicals.

Jay DeMoir would love to hear from his readers. Feel free to contact him via:

Goodreads: Jay DeMoir

Twitter: @JayDeMoir

Instagram: @jay_demoir

Email: houseofdemoir@gmail.com